Hi-Doh Hi-Dee Ha-Ha

A Journey to Where Everything Is, and Always Will Be

Tom Calarco

Illustrations: Erik McKenney & Mary Glasmeier

Cover Art: Mary Glasmeier

Copyright © 2021 by Tom Calarco

ISBN: 978-0-9651922-2-4

*To all those who love music
and understand the harmony
it can bring to our lives.*

About the Author

In addition to his fantasy novel, Hi-doh Hi-dee Ha-Ha, Tom Calarco is the author / editor of nine books about the Underground Railroad (UGRR) and the antebellum period. They include *The Underground Railroad and the Adirondack Region*, for which he won the year 2008 *Underground Railroad Free Press* award for "Advancement of Knowledge in UGRR studies, and *Secret Lives of the Underground Railroad in New York City*, which he co- authored with Don Papson, published in 2015. His most recent books are *The Search for the Underground Railroad in South-Central Ohio*, and a biography of antebellum reformer Orson S. Murray, of which the first part detailing his life in Vermont has been published at *Signs of the Times: Orson S. Murray in Vermont*. He has written for many publications during the last 30 years, including more than a decade as a stringer for antiques publications and as a classical music reviewer.

Tom Calarco

About the Book

For an introduction in the words of the author, visit:

https://www.youtube.com/watch?v=37AzNlOoxAw

Tom Calarco

Chapters

Chapter One: Practice, Practice, Practice!

Chapter Two: Puffballs & Gladiators

Chapter Three: Of Noodles and Tongues

Chapter Four: The Green Man

Chapter Five: Anywhere but Home

Chapter Six: Where He Surely Will Never Be Again

Chapter Seven: Windy Up Through the Leaves

Chapter Eight: At Geronimo's

Chapter Nine: Clear Water

Chapter Ten: No Longer Is It Never

Chapter Eleven: A Glimmer of Our Reflection

Chapter Twelve: A Wet Rescue

Chapter Thirteen: The Slobobslob

Chapter Fourteen: Down the Toilet

Chapter Fifteen: Sweetly Chirping

Chapter Sixteen: Remembrance of a Song Past

Chapter Seventeen: Happiness is Yappiness

Chapter Eighteen: The Spirit of the Flesh

Chapter Nineteen: The Magic of Edgar Allan

Chapter Twenty: Arrima

Chapter Twenty-One: Learning the Magic Words

Chapter Twenty-Two: Only Make Believe

Chapter Twenty-Three: A Most Ethereal Firmament

Chapter Twenty-Four: A Dandy Dog

Chapter Twenty-Five: Amen

Chapter Twenty-Six: And He Shall Rest in Peace

Tom Calarco

Chapter One

Practice, Practice, Practice!

The wind hummed through the trees and whoo-ed down a lane with houses graced by pillars, porches, and elegant entrances in the old part of Haneckhadee. It danced around a statue of an American Indian holding his bow like a staff and peering into the distance.

"How-now ohhh-wow woooh-phhew," the wind whispered the Indian's ancient chant.

Behind the Indian rested an aging white colonial house  with black shutters. On the second floor, ten-year-old Charles Patrick Paganono practiced his piano. His bangs tumbled into his eyes as his fingers stumbled. He pounded the keys and gritted his teeth. Then he grabbed the miniature bust of Mozart atop the piano and threw it against the wall.

"Good for you, old Mustfart!" he shouted.

There was commotion outside his room, and the door opened. It was his father.

"Charles!" his father roared.

Charles jumped and his hands fell off the keys. James Paganono, whose figure resembled a giant teapot, stood aghast. His face turned red, and his eyes narrowed.

"Oh my God, Charles! What's wrong with you? Pick that up!"

Charles picked up the pieces of the broken Mozart and put them on an adjacent bookshelf. His father folded his arms across his chest.

"Sit down," his father commanded.

Charles returned to the piano stool and his father pulled up a chair.

"Now you apologize for what you did."

"I'm sorry," Charles mumbled.

"I know you don't like the piano," his father said and took a breath. "But believe me when you grow up, you'll thank me for making you play. Let me show you what I mean."

His father nudged him over on the stool. He set his manicured hands over the keyboard as if attaching them. His hands seemed huge to Charles yet clean and smooth like a lady's.

"Listen to this, Charles."

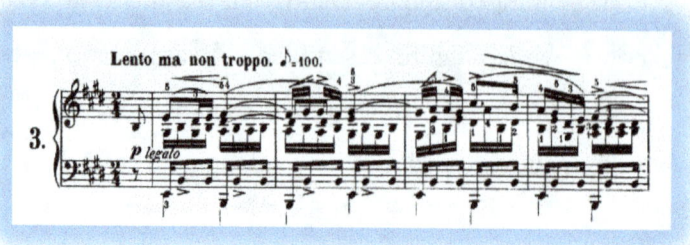

Chopin Etude

Delicately his father pressed the keys. How tinkly soft. The melody tip toed, pleading its sorrow. It made Charles feel as if he were saying goodbye to someone he liked but wouldn't see for a long time. He noticed his father had closed his eyes and looked as if in pain. And his father remained like this until he stroked the final note, holding it, slowly letting it fade.

"That's Chopin," his father said. *"The Etude in E Major."*

His father took a deep breath and removed his hands from the keyboard.

"Don't you want to be able to play music like that?"

Charles didn't answer.

"Music's a very precious gift, Charles," his father said, his voice softening. "No matter how old you get, or how bad you feel, it'll be there for you, all the time. You just sit down and play, and everything becomes all right. You'll see what I mean, someday. But you have to practice."

His father got up.

"Okay, let's hear your recital piece."

Charles moved back to the middle of the stool. His hands shook as he opened the sheet music. He set his hands into position. His fingers pushed down on the keys, then moved across. It was Fur Elise by Beethoven, or as Charles secretly called it, "Furry Lisa."

"A little more life, yes, yes," his father instructed. "Watch your legato. That's better. Repeat. Good. Good. Okay now, mezzo forte. Not bad. Keep up the tempo."

Everything was going well but the next part wasn't so easy.

"Now watch your slurs. Your slurs, your slurs! Stop, stop!" His father pounded the stool.

"How many times do I have to tell you? The slurring is very important. Do you realize your recital's only three weeks away?"

His father shook his head, then leaned over Charles.

"You've got to start getting this right, Charles," he said and hunched closer, speaking almost directly into Charles's ear. "I don't care how long you have to practice. Do you hear me!"

Charles didn't answer.

"Do you hear me!" his father repeated.

Charles mumbled a yes. His father walked out and slammed the door.

Frozen with sorrow, Charles went over to the window of the practice room that overlooked the Indian that sat in the square outside his house. Hawenneyu, or Howie, as Charles called the statue, commemorated the bravery of Hawenneyu, a Boogagoochoo Indian, who had helped the colonists of Haneckadee after a massacre. Charles had heard stories about it since he could remember, about the legends surrounding Ha-ho Hee-nee, meaning `place by laughing river,' the Boogagoochoo village reputed to have been at the very site of the statue, and Charles's house. Yes, right where he lived used to be an ancient, mystical American Indian village.

"Someday I'm gonna go where there's no music, Howie," Charles said to himself as he gazed at the statue. "Where I can do whatever I want, whenever I want."

For supper Charles sat alone in the kitchen wary of his bean burger. His parents were getting ready to go out with their neighbors, the McGregors. Their daughter Mindy was coming over to stay with him. Charles removed the slice of bread atop his burger and took out the awful sprouts which his mother insisted he eat. Quietly, he opened the door to the back porch and tossed the sprouts in the garbage.

He hurried back to the table. His mother was coming, her perfume preceding. She was wearing all this make-up too, which he thought made her look like a different person. She gazed at his burger.

"Charles, aren't you going to eat your supper?"

He scowled.

"C'mon, it's not that bad," she said. "To me, it tastes just like pizza. In fact, I make it with the same seasonings that go in a pizza."

He gazed at the burger and mumbled.

"Eat your bean burger," his mother said, "and then you can have some strawberries." Without whipped cream or cake, he thought.

At the sink, Helen Paganono tidied up. Once she had been a violinist, but a problem developed with her joints. Now she worked in a health food store and did volunteer work.

"You finish your burger, and then I'll fix the strawberries," she said and left the kitchen. Charles labored over his burger. It tasted like mush. Nothing like pizza. His mother must be crazy. He pushed away the burger. He'd rather eat the strawberries when Mindy came over because she would get the whipped cream and cake from her house.

After supper, Charles put on his Dandy ball cap, sat in his rocking chair, and turned on the TV. A program about an

adopted boy was on. He was talking to his father about what
he might be when he grew up.

"Some people just aren't good at some things," the boy's
father said. "You should try lots of things, to see what you like
and what you're good at, before you decide."

That gave Charles an idea. Maybe he could get his father
to see that he wasn't good at the piano and that it was a waste
of time for him. A rap came at the back door. Like a gust of
wind, Mindy came in. She dashed to Charles and stared in his
face, crossing her clear blue eyes and scrunching up her nose.
When not making faces, she looked like a pretty Olive Oyl with
never-ending dimples. She grabbed Charles around the waist
and tickled his ribs.

Later, after his parents had left, instead of having
strawberry shortcake, Mindy ordered a large pizza with the
works--extra cheese, mushrooms, onions, black olives, green
peppers, sausage, and pepperoni.

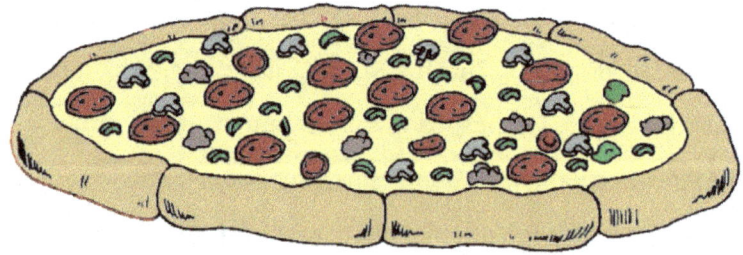

"Mmmm, is this good," Mindy said, as she sat with Charles
on the couch facing the TV.

Charles nodded, gobbling it down.

"How's your recital piece coming?" she asked.

Charles didn't answer and slurped some cheese.

"Not so good, huh?"

"The pizza?" he asked.

"No, silly, the recital piece."

"Ohh, Mindy, you know how I hate the piano," he said, while chewing. "I'd like ta, to throw it out the window!"

"Charles," Mindy said, and patted him on the back. "Believe me, someday you'll be glad you learned to play. Look at your father. In a couple weeks he's playing with the Windy City Symphony."

"So what!"

Mindy took her arm away from him.

"Well, everyone's excited about it," she said. "You should be too."

"My mother isn't."

"I wouldn't say that."

"But Mindy," Charles put his pizza down, "how can you get excited about something you hate?"

"Charles," Mindy said, shaking her head. "You know, Charles, I used to hate my lessons too. But one day I started to like it. Maybe you should try a different instrument. Maybe you'd like the flute."

"I don't know."

"Remember last year when I took you to the Nutcracker?"

Charles shrugged.

"You remember. You liked that part when the fairies danced, when the piccolo played. Maybe you should try the piccolo?"

Charles rolled his eyes.

"Well, what songs do you like?"

"I don't like any songs," Charles said, shaking his head. Then he stopped. "Well . . . maybe one. You know Beautiful Dreamer?"

"Beautiful Dreamer! Of course! That's a great song," she said. "In fact, I have a recording of it. Let's go to my house and get it. We'll get my flute and James Galway CDs too."

Mindy could've played her flute and recordings all night, but Charles became bored. What sounds lovely to one person might sound awful to another. Also, music is like a friend. It takes time to appreciate. Besides, Mindy had promised to read from one of her Oz books. They were so funny and took Charles to a place far away from home.

Chapter Two

Puffballs & Gladiators

The next day, Charles was as usual practicing his piano lessons. He had to practice every day ever since he had resumed his lessons four months earlier.

Yes, resumed. He actually had begun lessons five years before when he was only five years old!

Everyone was excited because he was so young and seemed to be doing so well. People were praising him and saying that someday he would be playing concerts like his father. At least at first. But he had to practice all the time and when he made a mistake, oh my God, his father would grit his teeth and huff and puff like the wolf in the old fairy tale. Sometimes when this happened, Charles felt like he couldn't breathe. And he began to have nightmares. In one he dreamed his father had a toilet plunger and beat his hands.

One day, he tripped going down the stairs, and they had to take him to the hospital to stitch up his eyebrow that was severely cut. His breathing problems worsened after this, and his parents took him to the doctor who said he had severe asthma. Believing that the pressure from his father was the cause, his mother made his father stop the lessons.

Charles's life was fairly normal after this. He had an ant farm, collected baseball cards, and followed the Windy City Dandies. His favorite player was home run hitter Nicky Noodle.

Sometimes he would go into the bathroom, and while on the toilet, imagine hitting home runs. Occasionally, in his bedroom, he'd sneak on his headphones which had radio built-in and listen to the Dandies in the dark, waiting for Noodle to bat.

But now he was in agony, trudging up and down these awful, endless keys. He thought about the worm he had put in his ant farm. For the ants, it was like a fight with a dinosaur. Yet they won. Charles wished he could watch them now or find an ant hill outside. He'd put bits of carob by it and wait. Slowly, the ants would come out. Then he'd poke into the hole with a twig and they'd pour out, like kids during a fire drill. And he'd pound, pound, pound away!

"Charles!" his father shouted from downstairs. "Do you like making those awful noises?"

Fortunately, it was Saturday and his father was leaving soon to go practice at the Conservatory. After a little longer he was relieved of his agony when he heard his father start his car. His father had been practicing a lot lately. He had an important concert coming up. His first with a major orchestra. It was a lucky break for him because the scheduled performer had hurt his hand. As far as Charles was concerned, however, the only thing that mattered was that it kept him away from his father.

Charles stopped playing. He got up and gazed at the picture on the wall of the famous lullaby composer. To Charles, the composer's thick beard made him look like a cough drop brother. With both hands Charles gave him double fingers and stuck out his tongue.

Charles went to his bedroom, grabbed his Dandy ball cap, and stampeded downstairs.

"I'm all done practicing, Mom," he said, grabbing some carob chips from the candy dish.

"Already?" she said.

"Yes, I've done all my exercises and practiced for my recital. I'm gonna go down the park."

"Okay," she said, "but don't be late for dinner."

He rushed out the back door and leaped into the yard. The sun and lilacs were exhilarating. He spun around, his arms outstretched, whirling like a tilt a whirl. Falling to the ground, he rolled on his back and peered at the sky. Drawn by the blue against white clouds, he imagined swirls of whipped cream fluff into a little girl with long hair that twirled into an Indian chief who transformed into a queen ant that became a flock of angels waving.

"Hast thou finished practicing perchance?" a familiar voice broke through.

Charles sat up and smiled. Mindy leaned over the rundown picket fence that separated their backyards. Her eyes beamed at him. Ever since Mindy was in a play about an Indian girl the Pilgrims thought was a witch, she would sometimes talk like that. He jumped up and ran to her.

"Gonna find some ants today?" she asked.

"For sure," he said, "and I'm gonna find a queen too."

"A Queen?" she said. "I don't know, Charles, they're pretty hard to find."

"I'll find one."

He watched Mindy, who stared up at the sky.

"Wow, it's really neat out today, Charles." she said, then gazed at the back yard. "Look at all the dandelions."

The frilly yellow buttons bobbed like waves among the grass. Though he didn't care for flowers, he liked the colors.

"My grandpa eats them sometimes," he said, "and so does my Uncle Vince."

"Eats what?" she asked.

"The dandelions," he said. "The greens, with oil and vinegar."

"Really? Have you tried it?" she asked.

"Yicch! Are you crazy?"

Mindy laughed.

"Let's pick some," she said.

Charles shrugged.

"C'mon, Charles."

Through a gate in the picket fence, he entered her yard. She bent down and plucked a flower.

"Look real close, Charles."

Charles knelt down. It looked different close up. Instead of one yellow ball, the flower was many tongues  opening towards the sun. She put the flower down and plucked a fuzzy white ball off another stem.

"See this," she said, holding it out. "It's a puffball. Here," she said and handed it to him. "Look real close."

Charles brought it up to his nose.

"See the parachutes?" she said. "Isn't it neat?"

He noticed a tiny network of furry strands supported by rows of hairs sprouting from a pod.

"When the wind blows," she said, "it'll pull the seeds out of the pod with their parachutes and send them into the air."

"What seeds?"

"Those brown specks, see," she pointed. "Look real, real close."

Charles wasn't sure he saw them.

"Watch this," she said and blew against the puffball.

A flurry of miniature parachutes was released, floating like snowflakes. Now, Charles could just about see the itsy-bitsy specks at the ends.

"See the seeds now?" Mindy said.

He nodded, and she blew again until the pod was almost bare.

"Who are the seeds' mother and father?" Charles asked.

Mindy looked out of the corners of her eye and grinned, showing her big dimples.

"Mmm . . . I guess you could say, the root, the roots in the ground."

She grasped a group of dandelions, bunching them together so it could be seen where they came out of the ground.

"All these flowers come from the same roots," she said. "And they're like parents. Eventually, every flower turns into a puffball."

"So when the wind blows the seeds away, they don't see their mother and father anymore?"

"I guess you could say that."

"Then I wish I was a seed."

"Charles."

"That's what I wish, Mindy. That's what I wish."

He got up and turned away from Mindy.

"I'm gonna go find some ants."

"Oh, c'mon, Charles. Let's look at more flowers?"

He turned and shook his head.

"No, I wanna find some ants."

"Okay, if that's the way you wanna be."

Charles opened the gate at the rear of the yard.

"Bye, Charles," she said.

He didn't answer. Instead, he followed a slate path to a small meadow. Known as "the ice yard" from a time when Charles's grandfather was a boy because it was used then to store mounds of ice, it was bordered by railroad tracks perched on an embankment. They led to a trestle, at the end of the ice yard that spanned the nearby Boogagoochoo River.

Charles picked up a large twig and looked for an ant hill. Past weeds and armies of violets, his eyes rummaged until spotting a miniature sand pyramid. Next to its teeny hole at the top, he saw an ant. He took out a carob chip and shredded it around the hill. The ant examined the morsels with his antennae then disappeared into the hole. A little later, two ants emerged.

As Charles waited for more ants, gnats buzzed and birds piccoloed. He wondered if the ants could tell the difference between carob and chocolate. His mother said carob was better for you and that you could hardly tell. But Charles could tell.

He knelt closer to the hole. He was getting impatient and wriggled in his twig. Jabbing a couple times, a couple more ants appeared. He wriggled the twig again, and this brought more.

Before long, a caravan of ants had assembled. With his twig, Charles nudged them playfully, when out of the corner of his eye he noticed a cricket slip under the grass. Carefully pushing the grass aside, he spied the motionless body of the cricket heaving. He snatched it by a hind leg and dropped it in the middle of the ants.

The cricket tried to leap away but the ants smothered it. Charles's heart pounded. An evil pleasure filled him, probably like what ancient Roman emperors felt when gladiators died in the Colosseum, or the way kids feel when TV wrestlers throw each other around.

It reminded Charles of the time behind school during the winter a few years before. Everyone was sliding down the icy blacktopped hill on cardboard sleds. He had laid face forward on a slab of cardboard and was about to go down when a whole mess of kids piled on him, forcing his face half an inch from the blacktop. Down they slid, and somehow he kept his head up just enough to prevent being scraped. He never was so scared, or angry.

As Charles watched the ants swarm on the cricket, a vengeance overtook him. He picked up the cricket and with his fingers carefully pushed off all the ants. After putting the cricket away in the grass, he took his twig and dug into the mob of ants, severing  heads, abdomens, and legs. Then he got up and stomped on the ground, grunting, gasping, squashing every little moving thing.

But when he finished, he felt awful.

Chapter Three
Of Noodles and Tongues

Charles practiced for hours the next week, paying close attention to his legato and slurring. Mindy had persuaded him to try to do well for his recital, because it would make it easier for her to ask her father to talk to Charles's father about changing instruments.

For some reason, though, his mother had started on his case: yelling about dirty fingernails, gum chewing, table manners, TV watching, whatever it seemed.

But then, the following Saturday, while playing for his father, he let loose again.

"This is not chopsticks!" his father shouted at his weak legato.

His mother, downstairs watching TV, shouted at his father.

"Peter! Keep it down!"

His father's face turned red. He shouted back.

"What d'you mean!"

"You heard me!" his mother called back.

His father charged downstairs.

"Don't yell at me!"

The shouting continued. In between Charles heard banging. The back door slammed. After the car had pulled away, his mother came upstairs.

"I'm sorry, Charles. Your father's on edge."

Charles glanced out of the corner of his eye.

"Who cares?" he said. "He doesn't care about me."

"Charles, don't be fresh."

Charles pouted and got up from the piano; his mother shook her head.

"I'm going," he said.

"Where are you going?"

"I'm going out," he said and ran out of the piano room and down the stairs.

Hurrying out the front door, he trotted to the railing that circled the Indian. At the foot of its pedestal, a plaque commemorated Hawenneyu's bravery over 300 years ago. Leaning on the railing, Charles scowled up at him.

"You ever gonna say something, Howie? Huh? No, you're just a stupid statue. That's all." Charles smirked at the statue, then left for the Center. Halfway there, he met a stocky boy with wire-like hair, pimply blotches on his face, wearing headphones, coming out his front door. Gino Negrino.

"Gino," Charles called.

"Charles," said Gino, who giggled as he slid off his headphones. "Did you hear what happened?"

"What?" Charles said.

"Ceybonia got his second Nicky Noodle!"

"Ceybonia got his second Nicky Noodle?" Charles repeated.

Ceybonia was Kippy Ceybonia, who was always trying to outdo everyone in just about everything. In baseball cards, Charles was his primary competition, but Charles did not have even one Nicky Noodle, who was also his favorite player. Except for Noodle, one reason Charles had done so well was because his cousin in far-away Windy City had sent him the cards he hadn't been able to get at home. But no one, not even his cousin, would give away a Noodle for nothing, even if he had more than one.

"Are you sure?" Charles asked.

"Well, that's what Georgie Kroochnik said."

"Did he see 'em?"

"I don't know. Georgie told Deezel Doubtfodder, and I never asked Deezel if he asked Georgie if he did."

Charles kicked at the sidewalk.

"Hey," Gino said, "here comes Ceybonia now."

A boy built like Gino came towards them. He had a spiked crewcut, and his chubby cheeks were dimpled in a taunting grin.

"Gee no. Charles," he said with laughter in his voice. "What's goin' on?"

"Not much, Kip," said Gino.

"Either a you wanna fireball?" he asked, holding out his hand and revealing two red balls the size of jumbo marbles.

Gino popped one into his mouth.

"Whatta they like?" Charles asked.

"They're good," Kippy said. "Try one."

"Yeah, and hot!" Gino said. "Mommalino, are they hot!

Gino groaned and Kippy laughed.

"C'mon, Charles," said Kippy. "Try one."

Charles reached out hesitantly. He didn't want one, but he didn't want his friends to think he was a baby. He grasped one with his thumb and forefinger. It felt sticky. He stared at it, before popping it into his mouth. He rolled it around with his tongue; it seemed okay, at first. Then the heat radiated. It was so hot! He spit it out and started coughing. Kippy laughed and Gino chuckled.

"You'll be okay," Gino said.

Charles's coughing gradually calmed, but before he had caught his breath, Kippy changed the subject.

"Wait'll you see what I've got, Charles."

Charles stopped coughing and Gino huddled closer.

"Then it's true, Kip?" asked Gino. "Georgie wasn't makin' it up?"

Kippy smiled and began to wring his hands.

"Wait'll ya see 'em?"

The boys gawked in anticipation. Kippy reached into his back pocket.

"Ya ready?" Kippy said.

Kippy pulled them out, and there they were -- two Nicky Noodles, side by side, their red borders shimmering and giving color to Nicky's smile. The eyes of Charles and Gino popped out as if they had seen a naked woman.

"Mommalino!" said Gino, as Charles gasped.

"So, uh, Charles," Kippy said, "how about you and me workin' out a deal?"

Charles didn't answer.

"Say, one of my Noodles for the rest of your first series?"

Charles felt like he wanted to thrash Kippy.

"Who knows, Charles," Kippy taunted, "you might never get another chance to get a Noodle again. Unless Gino here wants to trade you his."

"C'mon, Kip," said Gino. "Whatta ya nuts!"

Kippy shrugged his shoulders.

"That's my last offer," Kippy said, then changed the subject. "Let's go over to the Center. The Tongue's playin' in the ping pong finals."

"Sure," said Gino.

"And Charles here, can think about my offer."

Charles made a face.

"Let's go," said Gino.

Charles reluctantly followed. The Center was an old three-story brick building where a lot of neighborhood kids hung out. Inside, they found it packed with kids leaning against the walls and sitting on the floor surrounding three ping-pong tables. The matches were in progress.

At the middle table was the Tongue, a broad-shouldered boy with a pushed-in nose and shaggy hair. His fat, meaty tongue slid out, drooping, looping, and licking his lips. And every time he hit the ball, out it came. It was because of his tongue that everyone called him the Tongue. But his real name was Pete Pasquarella.

Not only was the Tongue a ruthless ping-pong competitor, but the toughest kid in River Valley Elementary. He was also the oldest, having flunked twice. Still, he was tough. The beatings he got from his father made him tough. And he proved it again just a few weeks before when he beat up a ninth grader!

Bam! The Tongue's tongue shot out as he slammed one past LaDonna White, a tall, skinny black girl in the seventh grade. She was a good ping-pong player too, but not as good as the Tongue.

As Charles, Gino, and Kippy squeezed into a spot around the table, Gino gave the "high" sign to the Tongue, who nodded but didn't smile. Despite the mean look on the Tongue's face, his tongue always made Charles silly. Every time the Tongue served the ball his tongue curled almost all the way up to his nose, and every time he returned the ball, his tongue would dangle or lurch at the air. Charles couldn't help himself from giggling and he put his hand over his mouth. Gino shoved Charles in the ribs and whispered.

"Don't get the Tongue mad."

Back and forth the ball and tongue continued, and then out of the corner of his eye, the Tongue noticed Charles laughing. He wasn't looking straight at Charles, but if you knew the Tongue, you could tell he was mad because his face started turning red. And the madder, the redder. Harder and harder he hit the ball. Then he missed an easy shot, and his eyes narrowed upon Charles, who couldn't stop laughing. Charles never thought he ever saw the Tongue's face get so red. Realizing he was in big trouble, he got up and ran out of the Center and straight home as fast as he could.

Chapter Four

The Green Man

A thick mist covered everything when Charles left for school the following Monday. He heard someone calling and worried that it might be the Tongue. But running out of the mist was Gino.

"Charles!" he called. "A wacko escaped from Wacky Valley!"

Wacky Valley, actually Green Valley Psychiatric Center for the Criminally Insane, was located in the foothills of the Peakaneenee Mountains about five miles north of Haneckhadee. The last time a patient escaped, the police captured him across the river behind Charles's school.

"Aw, c'mon!" said Gino, who had on his headphones.

"What?" Charles asked.

"The Chief of Police says the wacko's not dangerous," Gino said. "Yeah, right."

Gino's mouth dropped open.

"Mommali-lino!" shouted Gino, whose pudgy body jumped an inch off the ground. "The police are searching by the river. C'mon!"

They took off, running full speed. It was three blocks to school, and they were out of breath when they reached the playground behind it. They heard a din of voices and a hum that sounded like an orchestra of kazoos. Through the fog, beyond the playground, they saw a red light flashing near the river. They skipped down a concrete terrace to the playground. Moving closer to the chain link fence that separated the playground from the park along the river, they could see kids lined up and the red light coming from a police car. They spotted Kippy clinging to the fence.

"Hey, Kippy," yelled Gino.

Kippy turned and took something out of his mouth.

"Hey," Kippy said. "This is unfungusing-real. Did ya hear about the Green Man?"

"The Green Man?" Gino said.

"Yeah," Kippy said, "the guy who escaped from Wacky Valley is green and eight feet tall."

"C'mon, Ceybonia, whatta ya talkin' about," Gino said.

"No really, Gino. He's eight feet tall, and he's green. My aunt said so."

"How can he be green?" Charles countered.

"He is," Kippy insisted. "My aunt used to work at Wacky Valley, and she knows him. She said he's a giant who used to work for a carnival. She said they dyed his skin green and claimed he was a Martian."

Charles shivered at the thought of an eight-foot green man suddenly appearing in the mist. But Ceybonia was known for making things up. Kippy picked up something from the ground.

"You guys know how to make the seeds sing?" Kippy asked.

Gino and Charles shook their heads.

"Hear that whistling?"

"Ya mean that humming?" Charles asked.

"Yeah, that's it," Kippy said. "That's the song you sing with the seeds."

Kippy showed them the seed, which looked like half of a set of golden wings.

"You put it under your tongue and bite on it a little," he said, "and then you blow on it, like this."

Kippy demonstrated and made a shrill, whistling sound. Charles and Gino tried. Sure enough the seeds sang. And when a lot of  seeds sang, it was like a chorus humming. All three joined the seed chorus and turned their attention back toward the park.

"Hey," Kippy shouted, "there's the Tongue."

The figure near the riverbank was hazy, but it sure did look like him. Kippy and Gino called but the figure didn't seem to hear. Charles slipped back for fear of being seen. Then one of the policemen got out of the car and motioned to the person, pointing towards the fence. The person waved at the policeman and said something, and the seed chorus quieted to hear.

"Hair-ee Fiddlefarts!" the shouts filled the void. "Hair-ee Fiddlefarts! Hair-ee Fiddlefarts!"

It was the Tongue's trademark expression. He made it up the day "Leaning Head" Louie, their principal, came to class and Harry Bassarass passed this loud, long, disgustingly pungent barrage of gas. The policeman started to walk towards the Tongue, who took off. Kippy and Gino began shouting.

"Tongue! Tongue! Tongue!"

Soon other kids joined in.

"Tongue! Tongue! Tongue!" nearly all the kids were chanting as the Tongue scampered away and the policeman turned back.

The Green Man didn't turn up that day or the next, or after that. Neither did the Tongue. While it wasn't unusual for him to miss school, it was unusual that no one had seen him. Even Deezel Doubtfodder, his best friend, said he hadn't. All the kids were talking about it, and some wondered if the Tongue might've met up with the Green Man.

Charles's teacher Miss Heaney seemed not in the least concerned. As usual her back curved sternly; her wrinkles crisscrossed her face; her silver white hair electrified; her red nails were like daggers, and her eyes knifed hither and thither.

"I've got your spelling tests," she said, "and they're horrible. And Mr. Paganono," her lipstick-red lips mouthed her words, "I'm surprised at you."

A shiver went through Charles. He was sure he'd gotten a hundred. Miss Heaney pursed her mouth and began calling the names.

"Miss Cellanini."

A slender honey haired girl with a quiet snow-so-white face approached. Annette was a student of Mindy's father at the Conservatory, and Charles had a crush on her. Miss Heaney flattened her lips as she handed Annette her test. She looked at the next paper and shook her head.

"Mr. Paganono," she said.

Charles thought he detected a smile from her. His eyes moved to the test in her hand. He could see the red marks, and grabbed it. Turning away, he saw the minus seven at the top. He froze as his eyes devoured the words marked wrong.

Not one was wrong. He turned back to Miss Heaney, about to call the next student.

"They're not wrong, Miss Heaney!" he shouted. "They're not wrong!"

"What do you mean?" she said, then tore away his paper.

Kippy and some others in the back sniggered. Miss Heaney clenched her teeth as she looked at his paper. She looked up and dug her eyes into Charles.

"Look at your u's, young man," she said. "Every single one is wrong!"

She went over to the blackboard and made a u.

"This is how to make a u," she said.

She drew another u on the board. It didn't have the stroke down the side, but was still a u as far as Charles could tell.

"Your U is written incorrectly!" she said.

"That's not fair!" Charles shouted.

Miss Heaney stepped toward Charles and the wrinkles in her face wrinkled more. She applied her long nails on the side of his neck and dug in. It was as if Charles were in the jaws of a wild animal. For over forty years, she had perfected this hold.

"Don't you ever dare talk back to me like that again," she said. "Do you hear me!"

For an instant, she dug deeper before letting go.

After school, Charles went down by the park, hiking through the small, wooded area that connected it with the ice yard. The "Green Man" was still at large, and not feeling totally safe, Charles picked up a large fallen branch. Then he heard the click of a b-b gun. He moved towards the sound which came from the ice yard. At the edge of the woods, he stopped and saw the Tongue shooting into the air.

"Pop!"

Charles turned to avoid being seen but caused a loud rustle.

"Who's there?" the Tongue shouted. "Tell me, or I'll shoot!"

He raised his gun toward the shrubs.

"Don't shoot, Tongue. It's me, Charles."

"C'mon outta there!" he ordered.

Charles slowly stepped out. The Tongue scowled.

"Harry fiddlefarts!" he yelled and dropped his gun as he came towards Charles.

Charles held up the palms of hands and scrunched his shoulders. The Tongue grabbed him by his shirt collar and pulled him nose to nose.

"I should punch you out for laughin' at me, Pago," he said. "Ya know that! You little fiddlefarter."

He flung Charles on the ground.

"You're lucky you're too small to bother with, Pago. But you do that again and I don't care how small you are. Ya hear me!"

The Tongue turned and Charles slowly got up.

"Where ya been, Tongue?" Charles asked. "Everyone's been wondering if maybe you got caught by the Green Man?"

"The Green Man?" the Tongue hesitated. "Well . . . maybe."

"Really?"

"No, Pago, I didn't see no Green Man," said the Tongue, whose tone changed. "C'mon, let me show ya my hideout."

At the end of the meadow, they came to a chain link fence like the one at the playground. They squeezed under a section that had been pulled up. Down the bushy slope, Charles hurried after the Tongue, hopping over and around rocks and the large roots of trees. Charles was worried a rat might jump out. Though he had never seen one, he had heard that they were as big as small dogs down here. Trying to keep up with the Tongue, he tripped and fell. The Tongue, who was getting ahead, stopped and turned.

"C'mon, Pago."

They skipped over some big rocks near the river, which was the color of regular coffee. Charles noticed a dead fish bobbing alongside a beer can. The river was the color of regular coffee. Then they came to the base of the railroad trestle that crossed the river. The Tongue walked up to the concrete foundation that supported it. He pushed aside some bushes.

Charles followed him down into a cavern about fifteen feet in diameter and six feet high. A spotlight revealed Deezel, and Donnie and Ray Pepperoncini, huddled together.

"Where ya been, Pete?" Deezel asked.

"Just out shootin' birds. Then I ran into Pago here. Ya got me some food?"

Deezel opened up a brown shopping bag. Inside were peanut butter and jelly sandwiches along with some pizza Ray and Donnie's mother had made. All the kids at school knew about her pizza. As she said, it was *the besta.*

"So how d'ya like my hideout, Pago?" Pete said.

In addition to the spotlight, Pete had a fishing pole, a bow and arrow, a sleeping bag, a knapsack, and a battered old bicycle.

"Nice light, huh," he said, munching on some pizza. "I stole it last month from K Mart and my old man rigged it up so it would work with batteries."

"Hey, Tongue," Donnie asked, "can I try out your gun?

"Sure," the Tongue said, "but don't take too many shots. I gotta save my b-b's."

Donnie took it and went outside.

"Run into any rats?" the Tongue asked.

"Naw," Deezel said. "Why?"

"I saw some swimming in the river across from the power lines."

"I heard rats'll attack ya if you corner them," Charles interjected.

"Don't scare me none," the Tongue said. "I killed one once with my bare hands."

The Tongue laughed and the earth shook, and they heard a distant blare.

"Uhn Uhnmmmmmm! Uhn Uhnmmmmmm!"

"C'mon," the Tongue said. "Last one there's a dead rat."

They followed Pete, Charles last in line. The blare sounded again. Through tangled vines and bushes, they scrambled. At the bottom of the embankment, they felt the vibrations from the oncoming train. About ten feet from the tracks, they stopped. On their left was the railroad trestle stretching across the river towards the woods and hills; on their right, the passenger train rushing towards them like a snake.

"Uhn Uhnmmmmmmm!"

Everything shook as the train zoomed closer. Its racket was deafening, and the boys waved up at a blur of a man at the engine. Already waving in the first passenger car were a little girl and an old lady, followed by more waving people, faceless for the speed of their passage, all to whom the boys kept waving.

Charles's insides flip flopped. He couldn't believe such a silly thing could be so much fun. As the train sped away, they waved at a conductor in the last car who appeared smaller and smaller as he waved back. Then they jumped for joy, the Tongue plowing down the others as if they were bowling pins.

"Uhn Uhnmmmmmm!"

Chapter Five

Anywhere but Home

The next day Charles had an excellent practice session for his father.

"Not bad," his father said. "But you can do better. In fact, you must do better. Your recital's less than two weeks away."

Anger spilled up from inside Charles. He had been practicing so hard and thought he had made a lot of improvement. Why couldn't his father say something nice for once? As his father let down the lid over the keyboard, Charles churned inside. He puffed his cheeks and let everything out.

"I wanna quit the piano. I hate it!"

"What!" his father said. "Why? Why do you want to stop?"

Charles didn't answer. His eyes shifted around the room's pale blueness.

"I know," his father said, "it's those friends of yours, Pasquarella and Ceybonia. You want to end up like them?"

Charles lowered his head and folded his arms.

"No," his father said with finality. "It's out of the question."

Charles whimpered. His mind heaved. Instead of looking at his father, he gazed at the picture on the wall of the geezer who had composed the famous lullaby. He felt ready to explode. He got up and looked out the window.

"I don't care what you say," he said, then turned around and stamped his left foot. "You don't care how I feel. All you think about is your piano. Well, I hate it, and I hate you too. Do you hear me, I hate you!"

Charles dashed towards the door, but his father caught his arm. Charles looked back and screamed. "Let me go, let me go. I hate you!"

His father smacked him opened handed, his wedding band hitting him square on the nose.

Blood trickled, and Charles yelped. His father let him go, and he ran to his room. Slamming the door, he whimpered into his pillow.

Minutes later, he heard his mother come from downstairs, and then a gentle knock at his door.

"Charles," his mother said softly, "can I come in?"

"Go away."

"I just want to talk, Charles."

He didn't answer but kept sniffling. His mother entered and he kept his face in his pillow. She sat at the edge of his bed.

"Charles, what happened?"

"I, I don't want to talk about it."

His mother went and got a washcloth. She wiped the blood away from his nose. "Charles, did your father hit you?"

He nodded.

"Why?"

"Because. Because I hate him."

"What happened?"

"I, I asked him, if I could, could stop the piano."

"You stay here, Charles," she said.

His mother went downstairs. He heard her scream at his father, and he heard him scream back. It seemed to go on for a long time. Finally, the back door slammed. The car took off. His mother returned with a dish of strawberries and frozen yogurt. She brought in the portable TV and he stayed in bed and watched it the rest of the night.

After turning out his lights, he heard the car pull in. He expected more fireworks, but instead everything became extra quiet. Charles couldn't sleep, and as the night progressed, he thought about running away. The more he thought about it, the better it seemed. That way he'd never have to play the piano or see his father, not ever again.

But where should he go? He had only one grandfather and grandmother, and didn't see them much because his grandfather was sick and they lived far away. The only relatives he really trusted were his Uncle Vince and his cousin Roger. Though they didn't live as far as his grandparents, it was still over a hundred miles.

One way he figured he could get to their house was by train. He always had wondered what it would be like to hop a train. Maybe the Tongue, who used to talk about it, would go with him.

But he thought about the Green Man and that was enough to keep him in his soft, safe bed. He longed for the good old days before piano lessons when his mother and father took him out for ice cream, on picnics or to the movies, or just down to the park where they'd push him on the swings or merry-go-round. His father also played the piano for them. And all the songs, it seemed, were happy.

Charles closed his eyes. He listened to the creaks and groans the house made at night. He became drowsy and thought he heard whispering. He pulled the covers over his head. Maybe it was his mother? Or his father? He peeked out. The door was closed. But when he closed his eyes, he heard the whispering again. `Run away, run away,' it seemed to say. He threw his covers off and looked into the darkness.

Imagining his father's mean voice and angry stare, he realized how much he hated it there.

Quietly, he dressed. Then he gathered his headphones and ivory handled jackknife, which his Uncle Vince had taught him to use for camping. After emptying his piggy bank and filling his canteen with water, he put on his Dandy ball cap and headphones. He rolled up the rest of his things in a blanket and stuffed it in his knapsack. He took a deep breath and stepped out of his room.

Tiptoeing down the stairs, he heard one of his parents snoring. His whole body rattled as he crept to the back door. He turned the doorknob and opened it.

The sky had turned a paler blue, and already birds and crickets were serenading the coming dawn. Shuffling through the moist grass of the backyard, he thought he heard a bird singing: "I'm going, going. I don't know where, I don't know where. Anywhere, but home but home; anywhere, but home but home."

At the gate leading to the alley, he stopped and looked back. He felt like crying. Instead, he opened the gate and ran through the alley that led to the ice yard.

Chapter Six

Where He Surely Will Never Be Again

Into a field of darkness Charles moved cautiously. He wanted to find the Tongue. Mosquitoes whined; leaves crushed; the wind whirred; thoughts of the Green Man fizzed. Just ahead were the ice yard and the railroad tracks leading to the Tongue's hideout.

He ran across the ice yard and charged up the embankment to the railroad tracks. He looked at the sun's rim coming over the blue-black hills. Thunder rattled, the wind whooshed, and he thought of his father. He scurried towards the trestle below which was the Tongue's hideout. Across the river he saw the night lifting off the sleepy woods. Carefully, he stepped down to the Tongue's hideout. No light came from it and he called softly.

"Tongue," he said. "Tongue."

No one answered.

"Tongue, it's me, Charles."

Charles went inside but no one was there. Maybe the Tongue had gone back home, or maybe he was out hunting. Charles went back up the embankment. He could feel rain in the air, and could now see the details of the trees and the thick clouds in the sky. He heard a faint pop. The Tongue's b-b gun! It came from across the river.

Charles had never walked across the railroad trestle. He had always been afraid. The trestle walkway, which was only a couple planks with a railing, was uncomfortably close to the tracks. And the woods on the other side of the river were said to be the site of the Boogagoochoos' ancient burial ground, which had conjured all kinds of stories over the years.

Thunder rattled, the wind whooshed, but then he thought of his father. He stepped onto the walkway. It wobbled and his heart somersaulted. It must've been 30 or 40 feet down to the river but he didn't dare look. He walked faster, finally scooting to the other side.

Black clouds swirled, lightning shrapneled, thunder banged, rain burst. He hurried down the embankment for cover. In the thick woods he squatted beneath an evergreen. He shivered but felt better knowing that the Tongue was nearby. Turning on his headphones, he heard static, then an electric organ and bass guitar playing a song without words. Charles felt the beat. It wasn't that he liked it, but it comforted him.

"That was Green Onions by Booker T. and the M G's," the announcer said, "and this is Easy Ed Johnson. We've got quite a storm outside right now, but everything should be clear and sunny by this afternoon. Highs are expected in the mid to upper seventies. Sounds like it's going to turn out to be a nice day. So, here's the Wonder Man to bring it all in . . ."

Charles was getting drenched. He sneezed then took off his headphones. The rain poured, lightning and thunder continued, puddles formed. He thought of the Green Man, the giant so strong that Ceybonia said he once ripped off a man's head! He heard something, behind him.

"Aaaahhhhhhhhh!"

Charles jumped and screamed as someone grabbed him from behind. Pushed out from under the tree into the open and the soaking rain, he heard a familiar voice.

"Hair-ee fiddlefarts!" said the Tongue. "Whatta you doin' here, Pago?" "

Running away," Charles said.

"Runnin' away? You? A fiddlefarter like you?"

The Tongue laughed as the rain began to let up.

"What happened? Your old man hit ya?"

"Yeah."

"Really? That fat, old nerd?"

Charles put his head down and pouted. He looked up and realized the rain had slowed to a drizzle. He turned to the Tongue, who slapped him on the back.

"C'mon," said the Tongue, and they walked into a small field. The wind rushed by and monstrous gray clouds sailed overhead. The sky lit up and thunder rapped again.

"Hey, Tongue," Charles said, catching up to the Tongue. "You wanna go with me?"

The Tongue stopped and turned.

"Where?"

"To my Uncle Vince's? We could hop a train."

"Where's that?"

"Windy City."

"I don't know, I kinda like my hideout. Deezel and the Peppers, they bring me all the food I can eat, and I don't have ta go to school or have anyone tellin' me what to do. Why don't ya stay with me for a while?"

"But, Tongue, I heard they were gonna send the police after you," Charles said, then scrunched up his nose. "Awgh! What is that?"

A gust of wind had carried over a foul smell.

"It's coming from over by the power lines," the Tongue said. "You ain't gonna believe what's over there."

"What?" asked Charles.

"It's unfiddlefart'nbelievable. C'mon, I'll show ya."

As they hopped across the rocks along the riverbank, the smell grew stronger.

"It's just ahead," the Tongue said.

They heard what sounded like birds chirping but shriller. The rain resumed. The Tongue hopped closer to the river and another downpour began. He stopped and crouched atop a boulder, pointing over its edge.

"C'mhere, Pago," he said, waving him over.

Charles crept forward. He looked over the edge of the boulder and his mouth dropped open. The Tongue laughed.

"Isn't it gnarly?" he said.

"Oh, my God!" Charles whispered, shivering from fear and the wet rain.

Close to twenty rats swarmed on a dead body. Its face had been gnawed beyond recognition, an eye was missing, and an exposed hand was bitten to the bone. The rats were crawling in the stomach and out the neck. From behind Charles came a shriek. A giant rat perched on a boulder. Big as a dog it seemed, with ears reared up like a devil and pointy teeth jutting out. It leaped at him. Charles hurtled forward and fell on the slippery rocks. The horizon shuddered then turned shocking white. Charles got up, but a crackling bolt scissored down and flung him headfirst into a tree trunk that seemed to split open . . .

"Pago!" the Tongue's muffled voice echoed.

Charles entered a foggy cavern. At the end he saw a point of light, and he ran to it. Outside, he found a sunny blue-lake sky and a green field with forested hillsides in the distance. He continued to run, farther and farther into the countryside, his mind dazed, his body overtaken. Effortlessly he dashed, losing track of time.

Having no idea how far he had gone, he finally stopped. He looked out over a field of dandelion that extended to the high green hills. He turned back towards the woodlands from which he had come. There was no sight of the river or the railroad tracks or the Tongue. He also realized that not only was his knapsack missing but also his headphones. He was sure he had them when he saw the rats.

Walking into the field, he continued until he reached the foot of the opposite hills where he found a small brook. It beckoned him and led through a gorge. He followed the twisting cascade of rocks, shrubs, and vines. Birds piccoloed, bees glissandoed, and the stream fell over a high ledge, creating a great waterfall splashing into a pool. Out of it, a beacon emerged and formed a rainbow. It flickered as it transformed into a transparent Indian: his face weathered but healthy; his body muscular and tan; his head shaved but for a silver strip in the center; his headband sprouting three large feathers. "Ho, Charles," the Indian said. "Do not be afraid."

"How, how, do you know my name?" Charles asked.

"Do you not recognize me?"

"Oh, my God! You're not, not How Howie, are you?"

"Yes. I have come to send you on a long journey."

"But where am I?"

"Where you are not, and where you never will be again."

"But I wanna go see my cousin Roger and Uncle Vince."

"This can no longer be. Now, it is time to smell the perfume of the flower, sing with the insect, fly with the birds, and love like the rodent. You will come to learn much, little brother. But its full meaning will remain with the eagle soaring over the highest mountain."

Charles didn't understand, but something made him feel everything was all right.

"Will I ever get to my Uncle Vince's?" Charles asked.

"Be not afraid, the Great Master of Life will be with you."

Hawenneyu smiled at Charles, then turned solemn and stern.

"I have spoken."

Everything vanished. All Charles saw was mist, sky, and sun glistening. So bright it became that it blinded him. And he felt he was floating until he heard the voice once more of Hawenneyu:

"Hi-doh Hi-dee Ha-Ha!"

Chapter Seven
Windy Up Through the Leaves

Charles had become a nut-like creature stuck in a cushion among rows of others like him. A head without a body, with no arms or legs, the creatures were capped by long poles with feathery white umbrellas at their tippy tops. They sat on a hill overlooking a valley surrounded by stupendous celery green hills covered with quilts of yellow. Everything was so big. But where was he, and what was he?

"Charlie," a girl's voice called.

He revolved like a globe and came face to face with one of the other nuts. She had clear blue eyes and an impish grin. Something about her seemed familiar.

"Charlie, I'm so glad you woke up. The winds are coming. I think we're gonna go soon. I can't wait."

"What are you talking about?" Charles asked. "Where am I, and who's Charlie?"

She laughed.

"Charlie, what's wrong with you? You're Charlie. Don't you know me? I'm your sister, Windy."

"My sister? And what are we, nuts or something?"

"No, we're seeds, dandelion seeds."

"Seeds?"

"Yes, Charlie. Did you have a nightmare?"

"I don't know, but I feel really strange."

Neither did he feel ten years old anymore but younger, almost like a baby. He also could see so many shades of green now -- pea, avocado, olive, mint, jade, emerald, evergreen, and the very distinctive green of four-leaf clover.

"How did I get to be like this?"

"What do you mean?"

"I used to be a boy and, and . . ."

"Charlie, you've never been a boy."

"How can that be?

"It just is, Charlie. That's just the way it is.

"Okay, then what's this, this thing, growing out of our heads?" he asked.

"Our parachute. Don't you remember, when our mother told us about our parachutes, about how they could get us to the Gorge Ess Ness?"

He was still puzzled.

"We're lucky to be dandelion seeds, Charlie," she said. "Even if we don't get to the Gorge Ess Ness, then at least we can become pretty flowers and smell sweet like our mother."

"Yes, Charlie," said a soft voice behind.

He revolved again and looked up. A yellow face with long eyelashes smiled at him.

"Don't you remember, Charlie? It's important that you don't forget, because soon the wind will blow you away. If you don't know the purpose of your journey, then you'll never be able to get to the Gorge Ess Ness or bloom into flowers."

Charles who was now Charlie still had no idea what they were talking about.

"What is the Gorge Ess Ness?" he asked.

"I'll explain it, Mother," Windy said to the flower. "The Gorge Ess Ness is the blooming land, Charlie. The place all dandelions seek. Where everything is in harmony everlastingly."

"Harmony?" he asked.

"Like music, Charlie," she said.

"Music! Ick! I hate music!"

"But all dandelions love music, Charlie," Windy said. "Listen to this tune."

Windy hummed it.

"Oh, I've heard that before," he said. "What's it called?"

"The Seed Went Over the Mountain," Windy said. "You like it?"

"It's okay."

"You'll like it, you'll see."

Suddenly, their mother called out.

"Children! Listen. Listen, closely. Soon the wind will take you away. You must prepare your- self. As most of you know, you'll probably never get to the Gorge Ess Ness. So, the most important thing to remember is to land on soil near water. If you land in a dry place, your roots will never sprout and you will never bloom. Instead, you'll either dry up or be devoured by a bird or some seedeater."

Charlie cringed.

"Your chances of flowering, however, are good," she said. "Soil and water lie in wait all over the world."

His new mother's words were comforting. Still, Charlie wasn't sure how he was supposed to get to that Gorge Ess whatever, or even if he wanted to go. And he didn't want to be a flower. He looked around. How different everything looked. Bushes were the size of mountains, trees pierced the heavens, and the clouds seemed like soft pillows for the sun. Colors were more vivid too. So many shades of ever so greens, blues, lavenders, reds, oranges, yellows -- And everywhere flowers: massive yellow cups and towering violet stars, blue bells shaped like huge water pitchers, and tent-size umbrellas formed by clustered white vases. He didn't know their names, but they all seemed to smile at him.

Then a bumble bee hovered over. It was like a yellow plane with stripes and as it caressed his mother, the buzz of its wings played a joyful song.

Charlie looked at Windy who beamed back, but then there was a whoosh.

"Listen, listen everybody!" Windy burst out. "I think I hear the wind."

They quieted. Various birds chirped and tweeted. Then came a soft gong. A mellow whirr snuck up and puffed out a whooh that made Charlie and the other seeds exhale an "Ohhhhhh . . ."

They blew it out and it turned into a tune.

"That was your first breeze, Charlie," Windy said and laughed. "Wasn't that great!"

For the first time since he had that outrageous pizza with Mindy, he smiled.

More breezes followed, each one stronger, each ohhhhhhhh louder and more melodious. Soon all the ohhs, oohs, and ahhs echoed through the valley.

"Listen, children!" their mother called.

They quieted and heard humming like the sound of angels. It grew louder and Charlie felt it creep up his back.

"The West Wind, Charlie," Windy whispered. "Soon we'll be on our way!"

The humming turned into howling; their parachutes ruffled.

"Listen to that wind, Charlie. I think we're gonna go WAY up high."

The wind swayed them. In a delayed moment, a warped sound blew them away.

"Goodbye, children," their mother called. "Goodbye."

Charlie screamed and entangled his parachute in Windy's. Above the bushes through the leaves of the trees they were catapulted.

"Wow, Charlie!" Windy shouted. "Wow! This is great. This is . . . Wow!"

They continued upward, faster and faster. Afraid to look down, Charlie clung to Windy. As they rocketed up, he took a peek. The hills now looked like mixing bowls and the quilts of dandelion like cookies.

"I don't like being up so high, Windy. I wanna go back down."

"Down?" she said. "Why? Don't you realize we might be headed for the Gorge Ess Ness?"

They continued climbing. Now all that was before them were mists of clouds like sheer curtains. Then there was deep throated laughter.

"Stop, stop," the voices laughed, changing to a higher pitch. "It tickles too much; ooh, ohhh . . . stop, stop it."

The laughter of the clouds continued and turned into belly laughs as the flock of seeds passed through. This caused a great downdraft.

"Windy!" Charlie screamed. "Windy, we're going down."

"Hold on tight, Charlie," Windy said.

It appeared they were going to crash, but then they hit a patch of soft air. It buoyed them with gentle eddies, and they coasted down over a blue green lake opposite stretches of green hills. They were headed towards a town. Passing the lake, they drifted down over old houses and narrow streets. Gently, they landed on a street corner, some blocks from the lake. Charlie noticed that his parachute was torn but even worse were the motor vehicles. Engines vroomed. Cars squealed. Yownn. A truck belched black smoke. A bus sneezed. Fumes, horns, the blare of traffic was non-stop. Beep bee-eep!

"Whatta we do now, Windy?" asked Charlie.

"I don't know, Charlie. I don't know."

"This isn't the GORGE ESS NESS, is it?"

"I don't think so, Charlie.

They rested at a busy intersection where a sprawling, three-story brick building sat across the street. There was a stop light and one of the streets was one way. Behind them across the width of a sidewalk was a park with many shrubs and patches of grass.

"Are we ever gonna get where we're supposed to be goin'?"

"Maybe this is it," Windy said.

"This? This place?"

"It's as good as any," she said. "If we can get over to the grass there."

"But it's so dirty and noisy and awful and . . ."

"Stop it, Charlie! It isn't bad here at all. All we need is a little water, and we can grow up to be beautiful here just like our mother."

As if answering their call for help, a large butterfly with pepperoni wings, wearing a bright red baseball shirt and cowboy hat, fluttered down. The butterfly had a baby face and across the front of its shirt in white lettering was the word, Geronimo's.

"What in tarnation's the trouble here?" he asked.

"We need to get over to the grass there," Windy said. "Can you give us a hand?"

"Yurr durn tootin' I can."

Hovering over, the butterfly carefully untangled them.

"Who are you?" Windy asked.

"They call me Pepperoni."

"Pepperoni?" Charlie asked.

"Yep, I work for the Moplolapola tribe at Geronimo's Pizza."

"The Mop-lo-la-po-la?" Windy asked.

"Yep. An ancient tribe of American Indians. They've changed their name though. Moplolapola is short for "makers of pizza, lovers of lullabies, and patrons of the laughing anchovy."

"Laughing anchovy?" said Charlie.

"Yessiree," said Pepperoni. "No meat or **fish of any kind goes into our pizzas. That's why the anchovies are laughing. In fact, my job at Geronimo's is seein' to it that no meat goes into the pizzas. We don't eat meat, ya see, cuz we sabby it's**

wrong to kill and eat other critters like ourselves."

"Then why do they call you Pepperoni?" asked Windy.

"Because I can rustle up pepperoni without meat that tastes even better than the regular kind. It's my own, unique recipe. I've done the same for sausage and anchovies."

"How can you make pepperoni without meat?" she asked.

"It's the seasonings. But the main ingredient is our secret, 100-percent plant-based recipe. Tastes just like the real stuff, only ours is better for ya."

Charlie, already bewildered about being a seed and crash landing, wondered how a butterfly could make pizza.

"Ya have a hankering for some pizza, eh little feller?" Pepperoni asked.

"I love it!" Charlie said.

"Good. Seein' as how you're gonna be settlin' down here, I'll git it for ya anytime ya like. We're always rustlin' up crew pies, and we get to eat the fakes and the mistakes, so we have plenty extra."

"See, Charlie," said Windy. "This isn't such a bad place after all."

"Now to git you two over to the grass," said Pepperoni.

Though Charlie's parachute was torn badly, Windy's parachute was still fully intact. Pepperoni gave her a boost and she glided easily. He pulled up Charlie's parachute, which drifted slightly above the ground, and dragged him alongside when there came a gust of wind. Swift and strong, it blew Windy up and she was unable to stop herself.

"Charlie!" she yelled, "Charlie!"

Charlie's heart dropped as she rose higher and higher.

"Charlie! Char-lie!" she screamed.

She was moving far too fast for Pepperoni to catch her, and Charlie watched as Windy became smaller and smaller.

"Wiiiinn-ndy! Wiiiinn-ndy!"

"Bye, Charlie . . ."

Her cry was heard faintly as her parachute waved in the wind. Soon Windy was lost to sight, and Charlie could not stop crying.

"W-w-winn-dy ..."

With his antenna, Pepperoni stroked Charlie on the top of his head.

"It's okay, pardner. Don't you cry. Everything's gonna be swell as a pig roast used to be in the month of May. And your Uncle Pepperoni's right here to take care of ya."

Charlie cried even louder, and Pepperoni kept stroking his head.

"How 'bout some pizza, pardner? Isn't that enough to make your mouth water. Some delicious pizza right out of the oven?"

Charlie looked up and sniffled.

"That's better. Now, whatta ya say we head out to Geronimo's and chow down some pizza?"

Chapter Eight

At Geronimo's

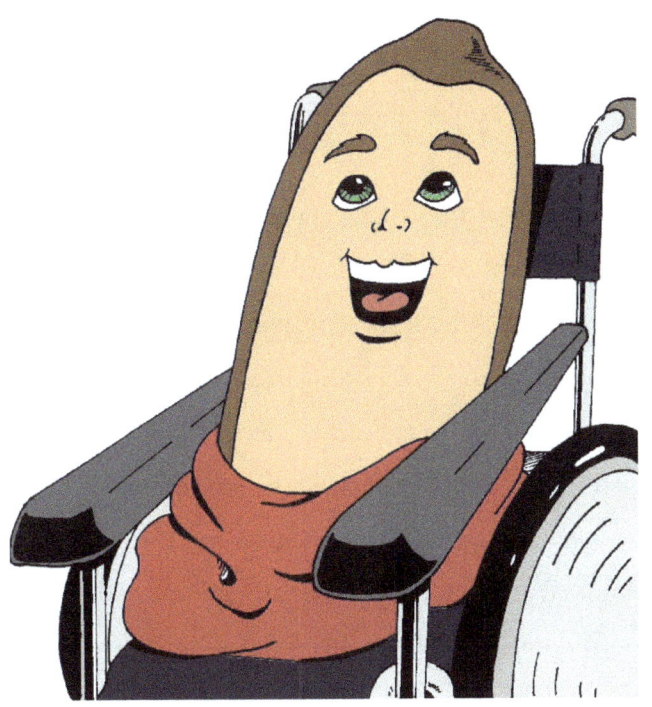

The prospect of pizza made Charlie feel better. Pepperoni grasped Charlie like a bird clutching prey and fluttered up into the sky. Sailing up, they floated past a lemon-lime sun. Charlie looked below and saw a city full of trees and clapboard houses with porches. Part of the city was situated on the slopes of nearly mountain size hills. As they coasted over the downtown area, he saw a long, stone square of stores and shops, almost like a mall without a roof. Pepperoni circled it once, then shot above the buildings until they were no bigger than salt and pepper shakers.

Before long, they landed on a dead-end street along a canal next to a small, gray-white stone building that looked like a converted garage. It had a small sign with red lettering, "Geronimo's."

Gently, Pepperoni put Charlie down. Then he took a miniature stick of pepperoni from a mailbox and shook it over Charlie. At once, Charlie became like a little boy without limbs but covered by a shell and sitting in a wheelchair.

Pepperoni also transformed, into a little old man. He wheeled Charlie into Geronimo's, where streams of heat from silvery ovens breathed from behind an L-shaped, formica counter. Adjacent to the counter an aisle led to the back, and behind the counter making pizzas were a large, ruddy-faced guy and a small, round-faced girl. Both had shoulder-length black hair, wore headbands, and red aprons embroidered with elaborate yellow turtles. The phone rang. The girl answered.

"Geronimo's Pizza," she said.

The phone rang again, and while the girl took the order, the guy smiled at Pepperoni. "Who is your friend, Pepper man?"

"A little fella I want everyone to meet," Pepperoni raised his voice so that the pizza makers and drivers in the back could hear. "And Rising Moon, rustle up some pizza for him right pronto. He's hungry as a buffalo. Ain't ya, Charlie?"

Charlie was not merely hungry, he was starving.

The girl put the phone down and leaned over the counter.

"Where did ya find him, Pep?" the girl asked.

"He fell from the sky," Pepperoni said, "and landed at the corner of Cayuga and Buffalo. His name's Charlie."

Pepperoni glanced at Charlie.

"This here's Falling Star, Charlie," he said.

"Hi, Charlie," said Falling Star.

Down the aisle came three drivers. There was a tall cowboy with a ten-gallon hat, a white-whiskered sodbuster with the brim of his hat folded up, and a guy who looked like the pizzamakers' brother. All three were munching on pizza and had money changers slung from their belts like six shooters the gunslingers used to wear in the old West.

"Hi, boys," Pepperoni said. "This here's Charlie."

"Now, Charlie, this here's Pilgrim," Pepperoni said, pointing to the big cowboy who bit off a chunk of pizza and nodded.

"This is Gibby," Pepperoni said, motioning to the white-whiskered gent.

"Hi ya doin', young feller," he said, patted Charlie on the head, and giggled.

"And this is Sagootsi," Pepperoni said.

Sagootsi, whose hair was in braids, nodded and waved his pizza-less hand.

"Ho," he said between chews.

"Your pizza almost ready, Charlie," said Rising Moon, who turned to Pepperoni. "How you like we make War on Pizza chant, Pepper man?"

"I reckon," Pepperoni said.

Falling Star leaned over the counter again and looked at Charlie: "You know what prayers are, Charlie?"

Charlie nodded.

"Well, the War on Pizza chant is our most important prayer," she said. "If you like, just chant along."

Sagootsi went behind the counter and faced Rising Moon.

Falling Star pulled out a tom-tom.

The Cowboys stood motionless.

"Begin, Sagootsi," said Rising Moon.

Sagootsi started to dance and chant. A few beats later, Rising Moon joined him as Falling Star beat on the tom-tom.

"Hinna no way hey-nay hear us say. Hinna no way, hear-us-say-ay, War on Pizza dough-uh, War on Pizza dough-uh."

They danced like regal birds.

"All together," Rising Moon commanded and the cowboys joined in.

"Hinna no way hey-nay hear us say. Hinna no way, hear-us-say-ay, War on Pizza dough-uh, War on Pizza dough-uh."

When the chant ended, Rising Moon opened the oven and the heat poured out. He shoveled three slices of pizza onto a paper plate.

"Now, for some pizza, Charlie," he said and handed the plate to Pepperoni, who held out the plate to Charlie. It had his favorite ingredients: sausage and green peppers. Because Charlie had no hands, Pepperoni fed him. Charlie took a bite . . .

Mmmmm! Was it ever good. He wished he could share it with Windy. He took another bite. Mmmmm, it made him feel better all over. Even though he didn't have arms or legs now, at least there was lots of pizza and he had lots of friends.

After Charlie had four pieces, Falling Star put him into a cradle. In her soft, high voice she sang him a Moplolapola lullaby.

> Ho, ho what tay nay
>
> Ho, ho what tay nay
>
> Ho, ho what tay nay
>
> Key oh kay nah
>
> Key oh kay nah

Charlie felt sleepy and slipped into a dream: he was Charles again and the Tongue was calling him a fiddlefarter, the other kids were laughing, and he was running away from home as fast as he could while old Mustfart and his father chased him with a big, fat toilet plunger . . .

Chapter Nine
Clear Water

Charlie opened his eyes and saw Pepperoni's grinning face.

"You woke up just in time, Pardner. We're gonna deliver some pizzas to our favorite customer."

They folded Charlie's wheelchair and buckled him in a car seat. Zooming off in Pilgrim's rusting mid-seventies Buick, Charlie never smelled anything so good as the aroma of the extra-large "Pepper Special" pizzas with green peppers, red peppers, yellow peppers, roasted peppers, cherry peppers, jalapeno peppers, pepperoncini, and pepperoni.

"This has gotta be the hottest pizza in town, eh Pep," Pilgrim said.

"Yessiree," Pepperoni said. "And it's right nice to have a pizza named after ya."

Pilgrim turned on his tape player which blasted Rollin' on a River. His huge body rocked the car to the beat.

"Get me a job in the city . . ."

Pilgrim squealed around a corner, burning rubber, and Charlie's insides dipsy doodled.

"Don't sweat it, Charlie," Pepperoni whispered. "Pilgrim might drive a hang bit too fast, but he knows his trade."

They screeched to a stop in front of a five-story apartment building. They put Charlie back into his wheelchair and hurried to the elevator which took them to an apartment on the top floor. Pilgrim rang the doorbell and chimes played "do re-mi." The door opened to reveal a young woman with waist-length red hair, a purple kazoo hanging from her neck, black pantaloons, and a green paisley blouse.

"Pepperoni! Pilgrim!"

"Howdy, Emma," said Pepperoni and Pilgrim.

"C'mon in," she said, looking at Charlie, "have some pizza. I need to talk to you guys. That's why I ordered the extra one."

"This is our newest pardner, Charlie," Pepperoni said, wheeling in Charlie.

"Hi, Charlie," she said, her hands in constant motion, her eyes aglow, "and what are you?"

Charlie smiled.

"I guess I'm a seed, a dandelion seed," he said.

Pepperoni took Emma aside and whispered something. Then they sat down to eat some pizza.

"What in tarnation do you want to talk to us about?" Pepperoni asked.

"It's something I'm working on with Dr. Karl. I was hoping the crew at Geronimo's might help. We need a group to play my Skratch Band. We thought you'd be the right ones to do it."

"I reckon we might," Pepperoni said.

"Good. Then I'll come down to the shop at closing time and explain everything."

After they finished eating, Pepperoni suggested that Emma show them her Skratch Band. They followed Emma to the back of her apartment. Pilgrim helped Pepperoni carry Charlie's wheelchair upstairs into a large room. It had no furniture and the hardwood floor was covered with all sorts of implements: soup pots, frying pans, sand pails, butter knives, mixing bowls, beer mugs, water glasses, coffee cans, key chains, screwdrivers, hammers, spoons, brooms, megaphones, cymbals, bags of sea shells, various bells, an electric pocket piano, and a genuine foghorn.

"The object," Emma said, "is to randomly shake, bang, rap, ring, or play anything for as long or loud or soft as you want. Watch me."

Emma picked up a spoon and started banging and clanging one thing after another; then she picked up a soup pot and bashed it against a frying pan. She gestured to Pepperoni and Pilgrim to join her.

Charlie watched as all three began tapping, slapping, ramming, slamming, swatting, swinging, shaking, pealing, pinging, butting, beating, bonging, crashing, and thrashing. He wished he could join in the fun, but just listening to the different sounds was a treat. If only he had hands to use, he'd even be glad to play the piano now.

Later, that night, it was a hectic scene when Emma arrived at Geronimo's. All the drivers were emptying their wallets and moneychangers, and the pizza makers were counting the drivers' pizza tickets and adding up their totals. The thirst built up after a hard night's work was being quenched by bottles of Li'l Leprechaun spring water. Besides the crew Charlie had already met, there were new faces: Roy, Gene, and Hop-a-long, who were drivers; Cochise and Silverheels, who were pizza makers.

After everything had been accounted for, everyone gathered around Emma who sat on the counter.

"What I'm going to talk to you about is something dear to everyone at Geronimo's, the preservation of Mother Earth," she began. "I know you're dedicated to a pure and healthy life, but this is no longer enough. If we don't do something fast, conditions will be so bad that little fellas like Charlie won't be able to grow up into flowers. And you know what that means? Without flowers, we'll all die."

"Yes," Rising Moon said. "As you know, we already install gas savers in our cars, use recycled packaging, and make only meatless pizza."

"Yes," Emma said, "those all help."

"But what difference does it make what a few buckaroos and injuns like us do anyhow?" Gibby asked.

"You shouldn't think like that Gibby," said Emma. "If everyone thought that way, nothing ever would be done. Every time anyone recycles a can, jar, bag, or plastic container, it helps. Every time we restore something old or go to a garage sale or have our own garage sale, we preserve the future; every time we plant a tree or use both sides of the paper, we keep the earth green. Ben Franklin said, `Be moderate in all things.' I say: Always use less and never go to excess."

"And that means less pizza too," Pepperoni said, "is that it, Emma?

"You got it, Pep," she said. "And we must be always on guard for fumes, hazardous waste, and polluted air and water. If we find problems, we must tell our local officials. If that fails, we must write letters to newspaper editors and call our representatives in government."

"I thought you had a notion to talk about your Skratch Band?" Pepperoni said.

"I'm coming to that," Emma said. "It has to do with Dr. Karl's Goodliness Principles. They state that any action producing harmony or beauty promotes the wellbeing of Mother Earth and all her creatures. This is where my band comes in. You see, Dr. Karl has devised a special sound system, which he calls his harmonic transformer. Broadcast at the proper frequencies, it cleans pollution out of our air and water."

"Is it like music?" Falling Star asked.

"Sort of," Emma said.

"Then music can save the earth?" Falling Star said.

Everyone laughed.

"Something like that," Emma said.

"But how can that be?" Gibby asked.

"I'm not sure," Emma said. "It's based on tests Dr. Karl did in his lab. But all you need to worry about, is playing my band. Dr. Karl and I will be in his helicopter transmitting your performance out over the countryside."

"So we're jest supposed to go up there and go loco and bang stuff around, is that it?" Pepperoni asked.

"Not exactly," Emma said. "It's important that you put as much love as you can into your playing. So, after you finish with the Skratch Band, you also might want to sing some of your own songs."

"You mean," Gibby said, "me and the boys can do Clear Water?"

"That sounds perfect," Emma said. "So, how about tomorrow? Can you do it?"

"Yes!" the crew said in unison.

The next day Geronimo's was closed. In the afternoon, the boys practiced Clear Water while the Moplolapolas sat and meditated. Because the Skratch Band was meant to be played spontaneously, they merely familiarized themselves with the various implements rather than practice playing them.

At supper the crew gathered at the weathered white and gray three-story Victorian house where the Geronimo's crew lived. It rested near the top of one of the large hills that rose through the center of town, and it provided a splendid view. For supper the Moplolapolas had prepared special pizzas.

Pepperoni wheeled Charlie into the dining room where everyone was chatting around a long table set with grass green linen and 14 golden plates. At the head of the table was Dr. Karl, a short middle-aged man with a considerable forehead, his hair stylishly groomed to conceal his receding hairline. Charlie was placed just to Dr. Karl's left, and he was followed by the smell of pizza brought in on a large tray by Falling Star. She was followed by Sagootsi with two more trays. They set them on the table.

"Take your seats," Falling Star said.

Everyone's attention feasted on her and the steaming pizza.

"You can take comfort in the knowledge that the pizza tonight has no cholesterol or sugar added, is low sodium, high in fiber, fortified with oat bran and vitamin C, and of course, meatless," she said.

The gang clapped and cheered, then went to their places. They looked towards Dr. Karl, who said grace.

"Let us pray. Dear God, we thank you for the billions and billions and billions of ecosystems in creation. We pray you bless them. We thank you for the sustenance you have provided us tonight. Please give it your blessing. We thank you for making everything alive, and allowing us to play a part in the trillions and trillions and trillions of life forms that ever were, are, or will be. And finally, Lord, we thank you for our great and wonderful Mother Earth. Amen."

As the others dug in, Dr. Karl spoke to Charlie.

"Hello. Charlie. Would you like me to put some pizza on your plate?"

Charlie nodded and the doctor put a fat square of pizza on his plate and cut it for him.

"I've heard about your incredible journey," the doctor said. "Don't worry. Everything will turn out fine."

Falling Star sat down next to Charlie and fed him. Charlie's first bite told him it was the `besta' he'd ever had. Everyone agreed.

"Excellent." Emma said.

"Deeee-lishous." Pilgrim replied.

"Yummarummy," Rising Moon gushed.

"Mmm-mmmm," Gibby intoned.

"Incred-edible," Dr. Karl concluded.

After a siesta, Emma and Dr. Karl went to the airport while the Geronimo's crew went to her apartment. By 11:30 everything was ready: Emma and Dr. Karl were cruising at 5000 feet, the Moplolapolas and Cowboys were in the band room, Pepperoni was in the next room at the controls of Emma's radio transmitter with the door open to the band room, and Charlie was sitting in his wheelchair next to him watching everything.

"This here's Pepperoni, this here's Pepperoni, do you hear me EarthSave? I repeat, this here's Pepperoni, do you hear me EarthSave?"

There was static and then Emma's voice.

"This is EarthSave. We read you loud and clear. Is everything ready, Pep?"

"The whole shebang's fit as a fiddle, and everyone's raring to go."

"Okay, Pep, turn on the mikes," Emma said. "Get set."

Pepperoni held his arm up to signal the crew.

"We're ready," Pepperoni said.

"Now," Emma said.

Pepperoni signaled the Cowboys and Indians, who launched into their task.

BIP BOP BAM BASH BUHDING BOOM BANG CLANG PANG PUM PSSSH CLASH KRRRSSSHHH!!!

It was loud noise, not music. Not what one would expect to be soothing. But everyone trusted the good doctor; he knew what Mother Nature needed. Suddenly, beneath the noise, the building felt like it was moving, and Emma's apartment began to rattle. They stopped playing the band, but the apartment continued to rock like a washing machine with an unbalanced load. It caused the band implements to give off a mellow ringing sound that echoed like the soft touch of cymbals. The house continued to sway, and Charley slipped out of his wheelchair and rolled on the floor. Then came a thundering boom followed by stillness and silence.

"EarthSave calling Pepperoni. EarthSave calling Pepperoni."

It was Emma. Pepperoni, who had crawled into a corner, got up and answered.

"This here's Pepperoni. We hear you, EarthSave."

"What happened down there?"

"I reckon it was an earthquake," Pepperoni said.

"Everyone all right?"

"We got our spurs tangled up a bit," Pepperoni said as he scanned the room. "But we's none the worse for the ride."

"Dr. Karl said to start singing *Clear Water*," Emma said.

"Pronto?" Pepperoni asked.

"Pronto!" Dr. Karl interjected. "Mother Earth's depressed. She needs something soothing."

The Cowboys quickly checked to see if the mikes were working, then assembled in the center of the band room. As Gene strapped on his guitar, Roy took out his harmonica, and Gibby positioned his washboard, Pepperoni put Charlie back in his wheelchair and gave him a mike.

"Croon along with us, Charlie, if you like," Pepperoni said. "You don't need a fancy voice either. None of us cowboys sing much better than a coyote baying at the moon. But it gives us a good feeling, so it doesn't matter."

Charlie had never sung before but now that he was a seed, he figured it didn't matter what he did. He cleared his throat as the Cowboys pulled up their britches and began.

All day I faced
The arid space
Without a drop
Of waw-terr . . .
Cool

Clear . . .

Waw-ter . . .

Pepperoni and the other cowboys sang in perfect harmony. As it thundered and started to rain outside, they were joined by the Moplolapolas and Charlie, who felt a few drops from where the roof leaked. Inside his shell he felt something squirming and this made him sing louder.

Cool.

Coo-ool

Clear

Clear-ear

Water

Waw-terr.

Gene, who had noticed Charlie singing, nodded to the others to let Charlie take the lead. His high-pitched voice was clear and in tune, and everyone else for the moment simply hummed along.

And way up there,

He'll hear our prayer,

And showhhhh . . .

Us where,

Ther-err's

Waw-terrrr . . .

Then everyone joined in:

Cool

Coo-ool

Clear

Clear-ear

Waw-terr . . .

Cool, Clear, Waw-terr

Hypnotized by the music, Charlie held the last note the longest, so long that he began shaking and felt as if he were going to burst. The Cowboys and Indians watched in amazement as Charlie lurched out of his wheelchair and rolled on the floor. He rocked and bounced and vibrated, much like a person having a seizure.

"Oh my sweet Jesus," Pepperoni cried.

Charlie split open like a clam. Everyone stared as Charlie, who had become the size of an insect, crawled out of his shell. White all over, he had six legs, and two antennae. As a seed he could  see just like a boy, but now he saw out of new eyes. Everything appeared as many dots of light like you see on TV when the reception is poor, and the only colors he saw besides black and white were purple and gold.

Chapter Ten

No Longer Is It Never

"Great mounds of mozzarella!" Pepperoni cried. "A baby cricket."

No magic pepperoni sticks had been waved, yet Charlie was now a cricket. "Zzzzeeezzzooozazee, Charcccazee," the cricket whimpered.

But the Cowboys and Indians only laughed.

"It's no time to make fun of Charlie," Pepperoni said. "Something plumb awful's happened to him."

"Zzzzeeezzzooozazee, Charcccazee. Zzzzeeezzzooozazee, Charcccazee," Charlie continued trying to communicate with them but they couldn't understand what he was saying.

"Call Emma and Dr. Karl pronto," said Pepperoni brought the microphone to Charlie so they could him hear better. Within moments they made contact with EarthSave. Dr. Karl listened as Charlie kept repeating the same phrase.

"He's just saying he's Charlie!" Dr. Karl said. "That's what Charcccazee means in Cricket Licket, the language of crickets."

How disorienting for Charlie now Charcccazee. A quilt of depression wrapped around him. He felt tired and crawled into a corner of the band room where he fell asleep.

When Charcccazee woke up, a covering had been placed over him. Despite the darkness, everything appeared as if it glowed. No longer did his `snowy' vision trouble him. He noticed a small opening at the bottom of the covering that he was able to slink under. Outside it, he saw that it was a cup that had been placed over him.

It was quiet in the band room; everyone had gone. He could smell pizza, and though he was hungry, it wasn't at all appetizing. Slowly, he crawled around the various implements of the Skratch Band now huge because he had shrunk so.

Instead of pizza, he had an urge for some grain or grass or weedy vegetable. He realized that he had to leave the Cowboys and Indians because his life had become so different. He also realized that they didn't understand this. Otherwise, they wouldn't have placed the cup over him. He wished he could explain why he had to leave, why he needed to go outside into a field and meet other crickets and learn their ways. But he was afraid they might try to keep him there.

Under a door he slipped to the stairway leading to Emma's kitchen. Going down was treacherous because each step was like a cliff and, unlike some insects, he didn't have the ability to walk on walls or ceilings. Instead, he had to jump down each flight. He managed this clumsily but without injury.

In Emma's kitchen a light was on, and he saw that his outer covering had turned from grayish white to completely black and polished like patent leather. The smell of grain led him across the floor to the foot of a massive cupboard. Strewn there were clumps of oats and nuts. Was he ever starving! For the first time, he leaped the leap of a cricket.

He bit off a chunk of the sweet granola. It was as good as pizza when he was a boy. He also noticed a puddle of water and quenched his thirst. How strange: He had one mouth for eating and another for drinking.

Now that he had satisfied his thirst and hunger, Charcccazee longed to meet other crickets. Across the floor through the living room he hopped, and crawled under the front door into the hallway. Cautiously, he approached the stairway. He looked down through the open space in the stairwell, but it was so far that he couldn't see the end. He wasn't sure he could make it. If he lost his balance, he might tumble down and break something. Then he remembered the elevator. Of course. It would be much easier. All he needed was to wait for someone to take it down.

As Charcccazee hopped through the hallway, he heard the most hideous laughter. It came from several directions. He stopped and looked around. But the laughter stopped, and he didn't see anyone. As he waited by the elevator, he felt as scared as the time he ran away and was worried that the Green Man might get him.

Finally, a huge pair of purple Converse All Star sneakers nearly stepped on him as the elevator door swung open and Charcccazee leaped in. In no time he was on the main floor and freedom.

As he hopped outside into the electric lit night, he wondered about the goodness of freedom when he didn't know anyone, had to worry about being stepped on, and wasn't sure how to get to a safe field. He figured it best to crawl into a crevice in the sidewalk for now and get a good night's sleep.

When Charcccazee awoke, he peeked out from his crevice. The quiet and empty sidewalk was being visited by a purple and black hopper. It was getting lighter but still dark enough for the streetlamps to be lit, and he had a clear view of a bespectacled, white bearded creature who hopped with a limp and wore a t-shirt with the inscription, `Be with ye brethren.' Impulsively, Charcccazee leaped into the hopper's path.

"Please, kind sir. Please help me."

"Goodness me, a poor, little clediddledeehopper," The bug pushed his spectacles off the edge of his nose. "What on earth put thee here alone in this burg, crying like the lost wind?"

"Thy? Thee? What do you mean?" Charcccazee asked.

"Thee, laddie. What be thy name and what leadeth thee here?"

"Ohh. Well, my name is Charcccazee. And you're asking, how I got here?"

The hopper nodded.

"I hatched out of a dandelion seed," Charcccazee said.

"Amazing butterflies," the hopper said.

"But can you help me, sir? I used to be a boy and . . ."

"Come hither, lad," the hopper said and patted Charcccazee with one of his antennae. "Collect thyself. What aileth thee shall pass."

"But I was a boy. Really I was. Please, please believe me."

" 'Tis not that I dispute thee. But pray be calm. Permit me to introduce myself Professor Oscar Worthington Hopper, nature lover and poet, at thy service. Please, call me Professor."

"But, Professor, can you help me?"

"That depends upon the nature of thy request."

"Help me become a boy again."

"A boy? Me lad, such things only luck and pluck can determine."

"But can't I ever become a boy again?"

"Perchance. If thou dost reach All-the-Time."

"All-the-Time?"

"A place where music endeth never, and all be so full of ease, nevereverwas no longer be."

This puzzled Charcccazee, and he changed the subject.

"What are you anyway, Professor? You don't really look like a cricket and the way you hop is . . ."

"Ay, lad, thy powers of observation be good. 'Tis true. Me father was a grasshopper; me mother, a cricket. Thus, I am what some might call a mongrel, a mixed breed, or a mulatto, though in actuality I am a hybrid -- an improved form of both. The reason I limp is that long ago, a nasty boy snatched me up and broke my leg and threw me into a swarm of ants. 'Twas only because the boy went mad and killed the ants that I stand here before thee."

Charcccazee thought that sounded familiar.

"Oh, and what are you a Professor of?"

"Of many and sundry things. But I have removed myself from the profession, to devote myself to search for All-the-Time."

"Is this All-the-Time far away?" Charcccazee asked.

" 'Tis hard to say," the Professor said. "Some believe 'tis just before one's nose, others beyond our most fanciful imaginings. Wouldst thou wish to join me?"

"Join you? Are you sure, it's okay?"

" 'Twill be my pleasure. Now, we needs must take leave of this city forthwith and find a safe haven."

Charcccazee followed the Professor across the traffic less streets, up huge concrete hills, through backyards, past several fresh streams brimming downhill. The hours passed and the day was quite awake by the time they rested underneath a huge boulder that overlooked a green valley with rolling hills.

"It bespeaketh of paradise, doth it not, lad," said the Professor breathing in the view. "But a realm more heavenly awaiteth, that I will pledge."

After a short rest, they headed through the field and stopped at the edge of the woods not far from a small stream, settling under ferns beneath an evergreen tree. At once, they gathered the necessary ingredients for the Professor's own hot and spicy dandelion stew: one dandelion, of course; chunks of wild onion; pods of peppergrass; bits of sour grass; pieces of burdock and thistle stalks; and finally chunks of Day Lily hearts.

The sun was setting when they sat down to eat. Already, Charcccazee was getting used to being a cricket and he found the stew quite satisfying and delicious. He also had made some wondrous discoveries about the abilities of his antennae. Not only could he use them to feel things like human hands, but they could sense emotions and other strange vibrations that he had never known before.

At the end of the meal, the Professor prepared some peppermint tea and honey cakes. The sun had fallen, and one by one the stars came out, along with the songs of unseen hoppers. Soon, the constellations sparkled in their configurations.

"'Tis time thou learnest to sing, laddie," the Professor said. "Tis the chief occupation of all hoppers. Tonight thou shalt learn how to make that resonant tone which shall be thy most precious possession."

The prospect filled Charcccazee with anticipation, for he had thoroughly enjoyed singing as a seed. But he was anxious to find All-the-Time so he could become a boy again.

"And then, after that," Charcccazee asked, "you'll take me to All-the-Time so I can become a boy again?"

"In time, lad. Crickets liveth not nearly so long as little boys. And if thou art unable to become a boy again, the niceties of singing must be acquired. Only in this manner canst thou attract a mate."

As the Professor took out some sheet music, Charcccazee felt like a boy again.

"This may astonish thee, Charcccazee, but a part of thine own body is a musical instrument. Lift thy wings."

Charcccazee did so.

"Now drop them."

To Charcccazee's surprise it sounded almost as if he had banged his hand on a piano keyboard.

"Now raise thy wing covers," the Professor said. "Atop are thy bars and below thy mallets."

Charcccazee saw that on the inside of his wing covers were little balls and beneath them what looked like a xylophone.

"When thy covers rise and fall, they strike thy musical bars. 'Tis how we make music."

The Professor showed him how to play simple tunes using the sheet music. Charcccazee found it awkward at first, but soon it came as naturally as taking a drink of water. After the lesson, it was time for the Professor to perform his own song.

"For us, nightfall is the most precious part of day," the Professor said. "For 'tis the time we sing our heartfelt songs. May I be favored by thine accompaniment?"

The Professor handed him some music. After taking deep breaths, the Professor tucked in his shirt.

"Thy understanding of me song may be lacking, but always remember: 'Tis the music which most matters."

He looked off in the distance. His chest expanded as he breathed deeply. He raised his wing covers.

> I've longed
>
> so many years
>
> for that heartfelt song,

flower-scented tears,

flower-scented tears.

The Professor's voice blended with the harmony of their instruments.

Melodies of golden halos,

daffodils and lilacs swaying,

the breeze

and me playing,

stars above,

even monsters preying.

So when

thy mistress

cometh in

that sweetest of duets,

nevereverwas

no longer be.

For 'tis now

which means forever,

so no longer is it

never.

Nevereverwas

no longer be.

Nevereverwas

No longer beeeeee!

Charcccazee was amazed how wonderful a singer the
Professor was; how sweet, sad, and peaceful his song made him

feel. The Professor said nothing more about his music. Instead, he suggested that Charcccazee listen to the songs of the surrounding hoppers, contemplate on the stars above, and feel the passing vibrations.

Charcccazee watched, waited, and listened. In addition to the hoppers, he also heard the most eerie sounds: the hoot of the owl, the squeal of the bat, the yelp of the wolf, the croak of the frogs.

Above, the crescent moon reflected its pale-yellow light and the stars shimmered. For a moment Charcccazee felt like Charles again, listening by his window on a summer night, feeling the touch of the air, watching for stars shooting across the awesome, bedazzling horizon. It wasn't long before he was fast asleep.

Chapter Eleven

A Glimmer of Our Reflection

"Charcccazee, Charcccazee," the Professor roused him. "Arise, child, arise!"

Fires of violet crawled up the black horizon and a succession of notes, wails, and singing had revived the woodland.

"Is it not beautiful, Charcccazee?" the Professor said.

"What?"

"The Delius. Take note of its yearning. Thou shalt learn much from the Delius."

Like the love call of a lonesome spirit, the bird seemed to plead to an ethereal power. As the sun's light renewed the marsh, the Delius's song enchanted the purple and yellow Flag Irises, made the white Cat tails frizz, woke the Marsh Marigold from a butter yellow dream, and took off the gold Ladies' Slippers, tickling their feet. Its woe woke other birds who tried to imitate it. Soon their poor imitations drowned out the Delius.

Later, the Professor taught Charcccazee about the uses and history of flowers like the purple clusters of Ironweed, the creeping Violet, and the lace white Fairy Wand. He was telling

Charcccazee the legend of the latter, which once was a magic wand, when another cricket called.

"Why, if it isn't my man," a thin cricket called.

The Professor turned and rubbed his antennae in surprise.

"Fred," said the Professor, looking surprised. "What bringest thee hither?"

"Hither?"

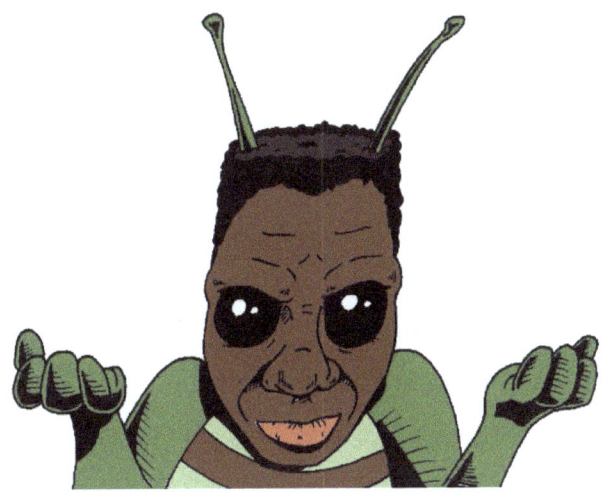

"To this heartland, whither lieth All-the-Time just yonder?"

"What's wrong with you, Oscar? Don't you know where you're at?"

"On the road to All-the-Time."

"You musta been goin' in circles, Oscar," Fred said and laughed. "Cuz you're practically in your own backyard."

"Alack, how can it be?"

"Forget it, Oscar. What you should be worried about is your old lady. What's wrong with you, anyway, goin' off and leavin' her like that? She's been worried sick over you."

"I proffered her a complete explanation. She could have chosen to join me."

"To where? Some place that might not even be, with some guy who's not sure where he's goin' and is always off poeticizin'?"

The Professor made a face.

"If I was you, Oscar," Fred said. "I'd get off my behind and get over to see her."

"A cricket's dignity must be preserved. I cannot retreat without some glimpse of All-the-Time."

"Well, come over to my place then. You can sleep on it. I just got a haul of fresh watermelon."

"Zounds! Watermelon?!" the Professor said. "You have me convinced."

Fred laughed.

"Then let's get busy. I'll make some chamomile tea, and we'll have a nice big dandelion salad with mushrooms and lemon tahini dressing. How does that sound, Oscar?"

"A nutritional feast," the Professor said.

Charcccazee followed them with relish. He was eager for some watermelon. They hopped through the meadow, the sun growing brighter. Passing throngs of bees and butterflies, they came to a sea of lavender clover. They stopped and sucked on its sweetness and became drunk on its nectar.

Their progress slowed along the endless grove leading to the edge of the forest. When they left the clover, they entered the canopy of the forest. A short way in, they sniffed a bitter, chemical odor that cleared their heads, and felt the earth rumble, drums hitting a military beat, rhythmic basses, rolling snares . . .

Bum bum!

Dum, dada-dum-dum-dum.

Bum bumm!

Dum, dada-dum-dum-dum.

The Professor and Fred froze.

"Come, Charcccazee," the Professor said. "Make haste."

They scurried into the underbrush, up a gentle slope away from the trail.

"What is it, Professor?" Charcccazee asked.

"Shhh, quiet, child," the Professor cautioned.

The drums grew louder.

BUM BUMM!

Dum, dada-dum-dum-dum.

BUM BUMM!

DUM, DADA-DUM-DUM-DUM!

The entire woodland shook as the poison odor choked the air. From above, behind thick foliage, Charcccazee watched the objects of their fear, a regiment of huge, oily, purple ants, whose gleaming, sickle-like mandibles armed with so many knife-like teeth were nearly the length of their bodies. In perfect step their six legs marched along.

BUM BUM

DUM, DADA-DUM-DUM-DUM!

BUM BUM

DUM, DADA-DUM-DUM-DUM!!

Suddenly, they heard a rustle behind them, and three ants stepped out of a clump of grass. The ants' heads bobbed; their mandibles gnashed at the air.

"Freeze," shouted one of the ants. "You are under arrest."

Fred and the Professor leaped, with Charcccazee hanging onto both of them. Down they came, only to smell more ants coming from the other way.

"We better separate," Fred said. "Here, take my lilac scent and sprinkle it on you and the boy. I'll take them the other way and put some moves on 'um."

Fred and the Professor gripped each other in farewell. Then they jumped in opposite directions, the Professor taking Charcccazee, Fred hopping above the grass.

"Hey man!" Fred yelled. "Right here, baby, right here!"

The Professor and Charcccazee crept away. Their hearts pumped furiously as they climbed the hill overlooking the trail. They crawled as fast as they could, the Professor sometimes dragging Charcccazee who was out of breath. When the smell of the ants finally vanished, they slowed. By then they were near the hilltop and exhausted.

Upon a stone near the edge of the cliff, they rested. The decoy had worked. But Fred was nowhere to be seen.

The next morning the Professor and Charcccazee went down the hill. They were quite shaken. The Professor had also begun to worry about his girlfriend Elizabeth. Perhaps she had been captured by the ants too. He figured he'd better go to her before it was too late.

They followed the brook that passed by Fred's home. It emptied into a stream, not far from where the Professor lived. The rising sun awakened the peppermint that overran the hill where the Professor's deserted old mansion sat.

" 'Tis surely a sweet smell," the Professor said.

They hopped up to a huge colonial house whose paint was chipped and windows broken. The Professor's abode was underneath the stairs. The smell of ants sifted through. It made them feel sick. The Professor called.

"Elizabeth. Elizabeth. 'Tis me, Oscar. Elizabeth!"

They crept in and the stifling vapors that had been given off by the ants made them cough. The house was in shambles: tables smashed, chairs broken, drawers open, things strewn everywhere.

"God in heaven! Elizabeth!"

The Professor's eyes overflowed with tears. This astonished Charcccazee, who had never seen a grown-up cry so openly.

"Elizabeth," the Professor sobbed.

"Don't cry, Professor," Charcccazee said. "Please. Please don't cry."

"Alas, my poor Elizabeth," the Professor said and dried his eyes. "No, we must not retreat. As a member of the ancient order of the Scottish Thistle, I, Professor Oscar Worthington Hopper, now pledge meself to the rescue of me maiden in distress, and I deign thee, Charcccazee, me squire and helpmate in this endeavor. To be sure, we can still save her, and Fred, if as she, he be so indisposed."

The Professor pulled himself together and led Charcccazee outside. Briefly, the Professor turned and stared at his ravaged home. Then they hopped down to the brook. The last thing Charcccazee wanted was to look for ants, but what else could he do? There was no telling when another ant patrol might come and he didn't want to be left alone. He was especially convinced after the Professor told him that ants considered young crickets great delicacies.

They followed the scent of the ants. The Professor told Charcccazee more about ants: that they depended mainly on smell and couldn't see well; that they usually forced their captives into slavery so that they could fatten them up before eating them; that when they were overstocked with fattened slaves, they'd hold huge public cookouts, during which they roasted the fattened slaves and which the unfattened slaves served to them; that when the ants ran low on slaves, they'd go on military campaigns to capture new ones.

The foul odor led them away from the river. Not far up the path, they came upon an abandoned red barn. In front of it was a mutilated cricket lying face down. He had only stumps of what had been his hind legs, which looked chewed on, and pools of yellow blood surrounded him. He looked dead. The Professor turned him over. Slowly Fred opened his eyes and smiled weakly.

"Ah-Ah Oscar."

"Save thy strength, Fred," the Professor braced him up against his knee.

"E, Eliz-abeth, Oscar, they've got Eliz-abeth."

"Take thine ease, dear friend."

"Oscar, my, my shirt. L-look."

" 'Tis fine. 'Tis fine, Fred."

His eyes closed, and gently, the Professor let his head down.

Before they buried Fred, they found a note in his pocket. It said: "Whoever reads this, please find Oscar Worthington Hopper and tell him Fred's been captured by Amazons and that they've got Elizabeth too. Tell him they're taking us to their colony, which is supposed to be close to All-the-Time. Tell him that the ants claim it's for real. Tell him he can get to their colony by way of an underground stream called the Formic River."

The Professor figured the scent of the ants would lead them there. So they set out at once, hiking through a number of vast meadows flushed with lily white Stars of Bethlehem and Star Grasses and up a good sized hill. Over the hill, they were led down to a river. Along rows of purple Loosestrife, they followed. As the river grew wider, the land became rockier, and they came to a series of rapids that fell into a pool.

"Alack!" the Professor cried. "The smell hath vanished. The entrance to the river must needs be near. Charcccazee, search for an entrance!"

Behind every bush, flower, and crevice they searched. The Professor thought there had to be a hidden passage that the ants had entered. But they found nothing and decided to rest. As they drifted off to sleep, a chorus of sighs sailed past with the breeze.

"Forget me not. Forget me not. Forget me not," the words hushed by.

Charcccazee felt a tug on his antenna.

"Gather up thineself, Charcccazee," the Professor said. " 'Tis the call of the blooming day. Hear the sighs?"

"Forget me not. Forget me not. Forget me not."

They followed it.

" 'Tis coming from that rock," the Professor said and pointed to a boulder covered by little cups of white flowers with golden centers, whose reflection rippled in the water in front of them. Using a lily pad, they cruised to the rock. Behind the flowers, they spied an opening. It smelled like ants.

" 'Tis our lucky day," the Professor shouted.

Taking along their lily pad, they slid into the entrance. They were barely able to squeeze through, but it gradually expanded until the cavern had become as spacious as a symphony hall and as cool as if air conditioned. Eerie purple light revealed formations that resembled towers or church steeples. Echoes murmured into the hollow dampness. It sounded like flowing water, and the smell of ants had become even stronger. The Professor's excitement increased. He hopped faster, leaving Charcccazee behind.

"Blessed be God, be God, God." the Professor called, his words echoing. "The Formic River, mic river, river."

Charcccazee hurried over and saw the calm river. Spontaneously, he began shouting too. "Hip-hip-hurray, hurray, ray."

Setting their lily pad upon the river, they continued to holler and listen to their echoes. "Charcccazee, arcccazee, zee . . ."

"Hark, ark; Elizabeth, lizabeth; Ahsscar's, Oscar's; on his way, his way, way."

As they proceeded along the river, the Professor shouted a poem, causing it to echo even more.

> The sun
> be neither more
> nor less
> than dust
> that rules
> the aimlessness.

> Like pigs who prance
> at weiner roasts
> Henry the Eighth's

breakfast toasts,

twigs 'neath which

crickets like to digest,

beans obliging

our stomachs

to rest,

or even

Holy Grails

melted down,

to pay

for feasting

at the Royal Crown.

Look around,

bright beams

shineth everywhere.

Everything's

like unto

thee

and me,

a glimmer

of our

reflection . . flection . . tion . . .

Chapter Twelve
A Wet Rescue

Hours passed as Charcccazee and the Professor followed the Underground River. The rock formations stirred Charcccazee's imagination. He saw one that looked like Kippy Ceybonia, another Gino Negrino, one like a hot fudge sundae, and another the Tongue's tongue. But more often he imagined the creature, whom the Professor said preyed at the gates of All-the-Time, the Beastosoreass, the dissonant servant of the Lord of Never Ever Will Be.

Gradually, the current slowed. After a sharp bend, they saw a point of light. They paddled as fast as they could. When they reached the opening, the scent of the ants vanished, and they floated into a lake flanked by bluish purple hills tinted with gold. So clear was the water that they could see the bottom and all kinds of fish.

According to the Professor, the scene was identical to a famous painting that depicted the valley below All-the-Time. He suggested they paddle ashore. As they pulled their lily pad onto the banks, a sparrow flew overhead.

"Go away. Go away," she said. "It's Dennis, Dennis, the Preying Menace. He's on his way, he's on his way. Put your pad on the water, and paddle, paddle, paddle away!"

"Arrrgggghhhhxoxxqkkccttzzzz!"

It was louder than a jet breaking the sound barrier. As they furiously paddled out on the lake, a green dragon like creature landed on a nearby bush. The creature had two wings that folded atop its body, two forearms like Popeye with gleaming saws attached, and four legs. It stared at them with its lighthouse eyes and held its forearms in the prayer position.

"Why doesn't it come after us?" Charcccazee asked.

"Because, 'twere to make the slightest contact with water, death would come at once," said the Professor, who chuckled. "But it mattereth hardly a fig, for we have reached the very gates! Dost not thou understand the import of that creature? Why, that is the Beastosoreass, the creature who preys near All-the-Time! All we need to do now is elude it."

The Professor outlined his plan to rescue Elizabeth and then find All-the-Time: They would go ashore at sunset; this would help them elude the Beastosoreass which had poor night vision; and they would douse themselves with lilac powder to conceal their scent. Charcccazee, however, had little desire to go anywhere near such a monster. Though he wanted to become a boy again, if it meant getting caught by the Beastosoreass, he'd prefer to remain a cricket.

All that paddling had tired him and he dozed off. Again, he dreamed about being Charles and of bugs so small he could squash them in his hands. In his dream he was telling Kippy the incredible story of his adventures when a banjo intruded. It was a song he had learned at school. He opened his eyes and saw the Professor rapping his wing covers to the music's rhythm.

"I know that song," Charcccazee said, remembering that the words went something like `the banjo on my knee.'

"Aye, 'tis a fine song," the Professor said.

Charcccazee could see no sign of the music's source but it got louder and faster, and a harmonica joined the banjo.

"If only Elizabeth were here," the Professor said. "Then we might do a little jig."

The Professor moved vigorously, causing the lily pad to rock. Charcccazee worried the pad might overturn.

"Stop, Professor. I can't swim! Please, stop!"

But the Professor didn't listen, and they overturned.

"Help! Help!" they shouted, for the Professor couldn't swim either.

One moment it seemed they were sinking and Charcccazee was watching bubbles rise above him; the next, he and the Professor were rising up with them. Soon they were above the water and sitting on something. It seemed that floating debris had carried them back up. Now the music was coming from an entire orchestra and the song was different -- Beautiful Dreamer. Charcccazee felt like singing, and used his wing covers.

"Beautiful Dreamer, wake unto me."

The soft mound that they sat upon swayed to the music as a violin soloed. Then the orchestra and Charcccazee resumed.

List while I woo thee with soft melody;
Gone are the cares of life's busy throng.
Beautiful dreamer, wake unto me.
Beau-ti-ful dreeea-mer, wake unto meee!

As the Professor clapped, up like a periscope came a humongous bald head atop a long neck. Its head alone was larger than the Beastosoreass and it blinked its blue eyes as it gazed down at them.

"Gadzooks!" the Professor cried. "Paddle, child, paddle!"

They paddled but the creature moved right along with them.

"Take it easy, little buggies," the creature said in a childlike voice, "I won't hurt you." They continued to paddle. "You're wearing yourself out for nothing," the creature said. "You can't get away. Don't you realize you're on the back of my neck?"

Charcccazee and the Professor stopped paddling. They looked up at the creature who broke into a grin.

"I want to be your friend," the creature said. "Don't you want to be my friend? I'm only a baby sea monster and I don't have any friends above the water."

"Then let us be friends," the Professor said. "But be advised, young sir, we hoppers are muchly known for our bitter taste."

The creature laughed.

"I'm not going to eat you. I only eat seaweed."

"What's your name?" Charcccazee asked.

"Walter."

"And where might be thy mother and father?" the Professor asked.

"Down at the bottom of the lake."

The Professor's mouth dropped.

"Don't worry," Walter said, "they almost never come up. They like the cold water. It's only babies like me that like to come up and look at the birds, bees, and trees, and listen to the hums and coos of the landlubbers."

"Perchance thou might help us," the Professor said. "Dost thou knowest of the colony of the Amazon ants?"

"Oh, my mother's told me stories about them. They live somewhere inside that hill over there," Walter said and craned his neck around toward the largest mountain on the horizon. "Do you want to visit them?"

"Ay," the Professor said.

"But isn't that dangerous for bugs like you?"

"My lady hath been captured," the Professor said, "and as a member of the ancient Welsh Order of the Thistle, I, Professor Oscar Worthington Hopper, and me squire here, have undertaken a Crusade to rescue her."

"Oh, I'm so sorry about your lady."

" 'Tis no fault of thee. But perchance thou canst be of assistance in another way. Dost thou knowest of the melodious haven, All-the-Time?"

"You mean where harmony is everywhere and All-the-Time?"

" 'Tis the very one."

"Yes, but I know it by a different name, the principality of Amram. Its Prince sometimes visits us."

"Doth he? And who may this Prince be?" the Professor asked.

"A musician whose music enchants even the deaf. I've taken lessons from him myself." "You play an instrument?" Charcccazee asked.

"Of course. You heard me before, remember? I was the banjo, the harmonica, and the orchestra. I play every instrument. Haven't you ever heard of a symphonic sea monster?"

" 'Twas thee who provided the music?" the Professor asked.

The creature nodded.

"It's no big deal. All symphonic sea monsters can do it. We're born that way. Maybe you've never heard of us before because we're almost extinct, at least that's what my parents say."

"Ay," the Professor said. "But of this Amram, canst thou tell us how to get there?"   "No, that's impossible."

"Nonsense," the Professor said. "If such a land exists, then anything might be possible."

"I'm sorry, but the Prince says he can only show you the way, and anyway, he comes only when he wishes."

"Canst thou direct our path in some manner then?" the Professor asked.

"No, I haven't any idea where to start," Walter said.

The Professor shook his head and pondered.

"Then, what assistance might thee offer?"

"None, I'm afraid," Walter said. "I'm just a baby sea monster, and only just learning about this big wide world."

"What about the Beastosoreass?" Charcccazee asked. "How are we to get past him?"

"I don't know, Charcccazee," Walter said. "I never go on land."

"Oh my God," Charcccazee cried. "My skin, Professor, my skin!"

Charcccazee's skin — as for all insects, his skeleton — suddenly began falling off as if cleanly sliced.

"Oh, I'm all slimy and wet and gooey!" Charcccazee cried.

"Worry not, lad," the Professor reassured him. "Thou be molting, and your new skin soon will dry and harden. 'Twill happen several more times before thou art full grown."

The Professor turned back to Walter: "Of this Amram, surely thou must knowest something more?"

"Well," Walter said, "they say it's where the air is fresh, and just over a hill. But it's never that far away. It can also be found near strawberry fields, close to lemon trees, or alongside a grapevine."

"How doth one know if one hath arrived?"

"They say you hear a hush. This is the signal admitting you to the orchestra. Then you can play any instrument you want, whenever you want, for as long as you want, and everyone in the orchestra is your friend."

"Is that all?" Charcccazee asked.

"In Amram," Walter said, "making music with your friends is all that matters."

"But what if the Dissonant One gets us?" Charcccazee asked.

"Let not such matters trouble thee, Charcccazee," the Professor said. "We shall elude that dissonant one, by that I pledge my troth. Then, we will be at the very gates of All-the-Time."

Chapter Thirteen

The Slobobslob

Walter found them a fresh lily pad, wished them well, and disappeared into the lake. The sun had nearly set. They prepared to go ashore. Knowing that the Beastosoreass perched in shrubbery, the Professor's plan was to stay in the open fields. To get there, however, they had to pass through the shrubs along the riverbank. And the Beastosoreass, known for its bushwhacking, could be very quiet.

The sky was deep purple as they crept onto a large rock. The breeze breathed off the lake, bugs sang, bullfrogs bellowed, and an owl questioned a crescent moon. Charcccazee scanned the tall shrubs, but saw only stillness, smelled only the lake. As they inched forward, the bugs silenced, the bullfrogs quieted, the owl stopped questioning. Charcccazee felt something crawling up his back, causing his antennae to stiffen.

"Arrrggghhhhxqxqkkccttzzzz!"

The Professor leaped into the air, clutching Charcccazee. Never in all his life had he made such a leap. But it was useless. Two green mitts snatched them like a baseball. For a moment, Charcccazee saw the glimmer of the

Beastosoreass's hideous saws before being blinded by its lighthouse eyes.

"I am Dennis, the Preying Menace, and I am going to eat you. Before you become supper, make peace with your baker, and pray he sends you, to your heavenly maker."

Closer to its mouth the monster brought them, then said grace: "Thank you, oh Lord, for this heavenly gift I'm about to receive from thy bounty. A-bugs."

The Professor let go of Charcccazee.

"Luck be with thee, lad," he shouted.

Charcccazee fluttered his immature wings and landed with a crash. Luckily unhurt, he hopped away, afraid to look back at the Professor, who made one last hideous shriek.

In the open grass Charcccazee hopped until he was far away. Exhausted, he noticed a silky, transparent covering spread across a bush like a tent. Interspersed were large clumps of rolled cotton. He reached out to the silk with his antennae. So sticky. He tasted it. Mmm, like cotton candy. He ripped out a piece. He ate more and more, and began to crawl farther into the tent. He began to feel drowsy. But it didn't matter. The Beastosoreass would never find him here. His vision blurred as he climbed up on a portion of the silk that extended like a hammock between two leaves, and he lay back. It was as comfortable as it was delicious, he thought and closed his eyes.

He dreamed of his mother calling him to get up for school and the piano playing. Soft, sad, deep tones. Rockmonnasomething, his father called it. So tranquil and soothing, it turned the sorrow into something sweet. But then a putrid odor intruded, followed by a hideous laugh.

""EUH, AHH, HA-HA-HA-HA!"

Ohh, did it ever stink!

"AHH-OOOH-OH, HA-HA-HA-HA!"

He tried to open his eyes but couldn't. He was tied up and the smell was getting worse. It continued to laugh. Then his eyes unglued. He screamed.

It was gigantic with two identical heads and eight bristled, pimply, spindly legs. Its beady black eyes fixed on him and its scruffy twin faces full of sores and scabs grinned. Its laughter was followed by a series of foul and cacophonous expellations which in turn were followed by more laughter.

"EUH, AHH, HA-HA-HA-HA!" the heads laughed together.

Charcccazee fainted. When he awoke, he was being licked by two slimy tongues that were like thick wet snakes.

"Ahh, my luscious tidbit," one of the heads said. "Do not be afraid. We are not going to eat you yet. We like our meat to age."

"But I, but I, but I could eat him up all by myself, Hawker," the other head said. "He's such a juicy little one, freshly molted and everything."

"I know, Willie," said the other head, who coughed and let fly a gooey slobber that slapped on another rolled up bug. "But he'll taste even better after we've savored him awhile. Right, David?"

For the first time, Charcccazee noticed a small, quick brown bug with long antennae at the creature's side. It purred and the creature began to pet it.

"HA-HA-HA-HA . . ."

As the heads laughed, Charcccazee noticed other bugs, perhaps as many as thirty, also rolled up in the sweet webbing. They were what he had mistaken for rolls of cotton the night before.

"David likes this little cricket as much as we do," Willie said.

"Yes, but don't you remember?" Hawker said. "We're having that plump water bug for lunch today."

"That's right! Well, let's at 'um. I'm too hungry to wait any longer."

Willie and Hawker foamed at the mouth as they tore away the sticky covering holding the water bug. Willie sunk his teeth into its neck and the bug squealed. Charcccazee closed his eyes, but could not help hearing the lip smacking, slurping, and belching. Then came a long-winded volley of effluvium like an orchestra of trombones with such a smell that it caused Charcccazee to faint.

Later, Charcccazee was awakened. "Yo there, little cricket."

He opened his eyes and saw that the two-headed creature had left.

"I'm sorry for ya, little buddy," said the bug, who had been spit upon. "But don't worry, when the end comes, it comes quickly. I think the worst of it is when it comes over and licks ya."

"Why does it do that?" asked Charcccazee.

"I think it's some way to season and tenderize us."

"And is that, that creature, some kind of spider?"

"Not just any kind," another bug interjected. "That's the Slobobslob. The most repulsive of all two-headed spiders, who's probably caused more pee-yous than anyone, anywhere, ever!"

Charcccazee started to cry.

"Don't cry, little buddy," the first bug said. "It'll be over soon."

"But isn't there some way we can get away?" Charcccazee asked.

"I'm afraid not. No bug has ever escaped from the Slobobslob's web."

"Listen, little buddy," a third bug said. "You'll feel better after you hear it sing."

"It sings?" Charcccazee asked.

"That's right," the first bug said, "It's got its own rock band."

"But I like the food even better," the third bug said.

"Yeah, if ya can enjoy it after thinking that, that disgusting creature prepared it," the second bug said.

"But it does feed us quite well," the third bug said. "The meals are not only delicious but huge."

"Yeah, that's so it can fatten us up," the second bug said.

"Now, guys," the first bug said. "You have to admit, though, that he will like the music." "What kind of music?" Charcccazee asked.

"The Mamas & Papas, the Beatles, Motown, Hendrix, the Doors, the Cream, Joplin, just about anything from the sixties," the second bug said.

Charcccazee gazed at all the bugs tied up in the web. Some were as big as cyclops beetles, others tiny as fleas. All were going to be eaten just like him, and there was nothing anyone could do.

The next hours Charcccazee watched as the Slobobslob tied up a poor firefly. It didn't bother with Charcccazee. Also, the bug named David delivered to each captive a huge chocolate ice cream milk shake, which they were able to drink through a flex straw and which Charcccazee found quite delicious. Feeling full, Charcccazee fell asleep again.

There must've been something the creature was putting in the food because once again, Charcccazee experienced a strange and vivid dream. In it, he envisioned a rock band tuning up, the electric guitars playing piercing chords. He opened his eyes and thought he was hallucinating. The Slobobslob was in the middle of the web and propped on its back. Two pairs of legs had guitars, another pair was on the keyboards, and the fourth on drums. Microphones hung from the necks of Willie and Hawker, who began to sing.

I know you're uneasy
And your stomach's kinda queasy

But I tell ya little buggies,

Don't worry 'bout a thing.

Just enjoy it while ya got it,

Eat, be merry, what else matters,

Let me show ya, it's so easy

To ler-er-earn how to sing."

Just enjoy it while ya got it,

Eat, be merry, what else matters,

Let me show ya, it's so easy

To ler-earn how to sing."

Gimme gi-imm-mee, Gimme gi-imm-mee

Bee-ee-tles, Bee-ee-tles

Gimmee Gimmee crickets, Gimmee Gimmee horse flies

Insect flesh, Insect flesh …

Hawker and Willie sang several more verses. After they finished, the Slobobslob laid down its instruments and approached Charcccazee. Hawker and Willie's eyes fixed on him and their long tongues slithered out. They hadn't fattened him up yet, so why would they eat him so soon?

"No! No!" Charcccazee screamed. "Please don't eat me! Please!"

Hawker and Willie laughed.

"Why shouldn't we eat you?" said Hawker.

"Yeah," said Willie, "you're not fat enough for supper yet, but you're just right for dessert."

The heads laughed.

"But, but I have to become a boy again, and if, if . . ."

The heads looked at each other with concern, then the creature backed away.

"A boy?" a squeaky voice came from below. "Did I hear you say boy?"

"Yes," Charcccazee said. "I used to be a boy, and . . ."

"Well," the voice interrupted, "it's been a long stretch since I came upon a boy."

A huge rear end of a black bug crawled out of a hole in the ground. It moved backwards and its tiny head turned on its body, revealing its huge jaws.

"Sorry about that," the bug said, tilting its head in Charcccazee's direction. "I'd never let anyone feast on a boy, or at least someone who used to be one. It probably would give him indigestion."

The bug untied Charcccazee.

"What are you and who are you?" asked Charcccazee.

"I'm an ant lion," the bug said. "My name is Bobby, and I'm a master of many subjects, including hot air balloons. I'm also lead singer of the Sloppy Bobbies, the group I formed with the Slobobslob. What's your slug?"

"My slug?"

"Your name?"

"Charcccazee. But everyone called me Charles when I was a boy," he said, then pointed at the Slobobslob. "Why are you with that Slob . . . ob?"

"The Slobobslob? Don't worry, he won't hurt you while I'm here. Like I said, we formed this band. But the main reason I joined up with him is to study him. I'm particularly interested in his eating and excreting habits. I'm trying to learn why he's so filthy."

Charcccazee gave Bobby a puzzled look.

"Yeah, when I was a kid, I was like him. And everyone called me Sloppy Bobby." "Sloppy Bobby?"

"You got it. I'd pick boogers from my olfactory organs, regurgitate in public, and of course pass a lot of gas."

"Why did you do that?"

"Cuz, everyone picked on me. That way I got back at them. Finally, I decided to study the Slobobslob to show others that things inside us make us do what we do, and that in order to stop these things, we must understand them. So, tell me, how did you become a cricket if you used to be a boy?"

Charcccazee told the whole story, and asked Bobby if he might help.

"Well, first of all, Charcccazee," said Bobby as he backpedaled forth and back, "I wouldn't be so concerned about not being a boy anymore the way humans are abusing Mother Earth. Though they're finally getting the picture, things still don't look so good. Now, I don't say it's hopeless. But it might make you feel better to know that the Animal Kingdom has started preparing its Underground World just in case."

"Really?"

"And just think," Bobby said, "you're no longer going to be eaten either. Doesn't that make you happy? You're lucky running into me like this, for I offer some fine things–bad science, badder music, and the baddest grub."

"Grub?"

"Food, boy, outrageous food. I'm a gourmet cook. Any of the bugs here will testify to that. My specialty is Refried Beans a la Bobby. By the way, any chance you might be able to play the sax?

"Sax?"

"The saxophone."

"I'm sorry, Bobby, but I used to take lessons when I was a boy and . . .

"Oh, so you do play something?"

"Yes, I took piano."

"Then you can read music?"

Charcccazee nodded.

"Great. Then you'll be easy to teach. Believe me, once you're playing, you'll love it. What d'ya say?"

Charcccazee didn't answer.

"Listen," Bobby said, "let me do a number for ya."

Bobby backpedaled to confer with Hawker and Willie. Instead of a monster, the Slobobslob now acted like a big, stuffed animal. Bobby took out a microphone and the creature returned to its instruments.

"Now, I want you to get into the groove," Bobby said.

"Groove?" asked Charcccazee.

"Dance, boy, dance. Shake that thing. You know, get down on it."

Bobby handed him a saxophone and told him that this was a special saxophone. Suddenly, Charcccazee found that he was actually playing it.

"I feel all-all all ri-ight," Bobby crooned, then nodded to Hawker and Willie to begin. "Weh-eh-eh-eh-eill, you know you make me want to shout!"

"Shout!" Hawker and Willie responded.

As the song grooved with the moment, Charcccazee couldn't believe the trembling in his legs, all six of them, as well as his antennae.

"Look my legs are jumpin'," Bobby sang and clapped his antennae.

"Shout!" the heads responded.

"Look my heart's thumpin'."

"Shout!"

Charcccazee couldn't help himself and started to dance around and around, as the bugs wrapped in the web squirmed to the beat. And before long, the music had drawn many bugs from the woodland, all captivated by the music and drawn to the web.

"Hey-Hey-Hey Hey," Bobby sang.

"Hey-Hey-Hey Hey," Hawker and Willie responded.

Soon everyone was joining Hawker and Willie in the chorus.

"Hey-Hey-Hey-ay-yay."

"Hey-Hey-Hey-ay-yay."

"Now we're cookin'," Bobby said. "Shout now. Jump up and shout now."

The music, the singing, the dancing, the swinging made the ground rumble. It grew louder. But suddenly, above everything, sounded a different beat.

BUM BUM

DUM, DADA-DUM-DUM-DUM!

BUM BUM

DUM, DADA-DUM-DUM-DUM!

Cymbals clashed. Everyone scattered. Bobby hurried back into his hole and Charcccazee hid under a leaf, as an acrid smell sifted through. Peeking out from under his leaf, Charcccazee watched the Slobobslob fill its poison sacks and sharpen its claws and teeth as columns of ants stretching as far as he could see came from eight different directions.

BUM BUM

DUM, DADA-DUM-DUM-DUM!

BUM BUM

DUM, DADA-DUM-DUM-DUM!

The soldiers halted within hailing distance and the drumming stopped. As they stood at attention, an ant came forward with a parchment.

"On this second day of June," the ant read, "in this year of our Queen Smellifluous, we hereby arrest you, the Slobobslob, not only for crimes against the insect world but for gross-me-out sloppiness that pollutes and defaces our beautiful landscapes."

"Come and get us," the heads yelled.

"You are surrounded by thousands of ants," the ant said. "You don't have a chance. In fact, it would bring us great pleasure to kill you here now."

"We'll never surrender," Hawker said. "You may kill us, but first we're gonna slaughter as many of you as we can."

"Yeah," Willie said. "Just feast your eyes on all that delicious ant flesh out there."

The heads laughed.

The ant spokesman turned and signaled with his right antenna.

"Let's get Sloppy!"

There was a trumpeting of horns and a clash of cymbals. The ants gave a cry and in eight columns stormed the web. Those in front stretched their bodies across it, making a bridge for their cohorts to walk over so they wouldn't get stuck. One after another they came. The Slobobslob stood its ground. It snatched up ants like an octopus with its long arm like legs, and Hawker and Willie bit off their heads and spit them out.

Charcccazee had to duck several times as heads flew by. The battle raged. The Slobobslob fought valiantly. But the sheer number of ants was too much. Finally, they swarmed over the Slobobslob as if it were a piece of candy and tied it up. While the ants inspected the web and took the bugs in it as captives, Charcccazee pretended to be dead.

"Hey, mate, look at this one," one soldier said to another.

"He looks dead," the other said. "Why don't we take him aside and eat him right now."   "No," the first soldier said, "if anyone finds out, we'll be in big trouble."

"C'mon," the second soldier said, "who's gonna find out? I'd sure like to feast on some tender cricket meat, wouldn't you? Look, he's recently molted."

As they dragged him away, an angry voice stopped them.

"Drop that cricket."

It was one of the Queen's Guard. Immediately, they put Charcccazee down. The Queen's physician came forward. Realizing Charcccazee was still alive, the physician took out some smelling salts. This made Charcccazee cough.

"Wake up, little cricket, wake up. I need to examine your reflexes."

Charcccazee opened his eyes and the physician poked him in the sides and looked at his mouth.

"Fit for duty," he pronounced.

They took Charcccazee away and chained him to the other bugs taken from the web, who in turn were chained to other bugs who had been captured earlier. Apparently, as the Professor had explained, they were taking them back to their colony to be their slaves.

Chapter Fourteen
Down the Toilet

As Charcccazee marched along, he thought about Fred's note, which said the Amazon colony was close to All-the-Time. Perhaps he could escape from the colony and find the principality as Walter called it. Then, if the Professor was right, maybe he could become a boy again.

Crossing a meadow, they marched down into a valley with several streams that ran along the foot of a chain of small furry mountains. After floating across the streams on leaves, they hiked up one of the mountains. A third of the way, they entered a tunnel and came to an underground stream that smelled like the Formic River. Using their leaf rafts again, they coasted. The bugs who had been captured began to sing. Then one took the lead. His words echoed hauntingly in the tunnel.

Oh, what a beautiful city.
Ohhh, what a beautiful city
Ohhh, what a beautiful city
Twelve gates to the city, Ha-ah-lay-loo.

Where, Charcccazee wondered, was this city? It dawned on him. Ever since he had run away, everyone it seemed was trying to reach some wonderful, distant musical place. While it had various names, he wondered if it might actually be the same place.

Finally, they came to a large cavern lit by purple lights where they docked. Through a tunnel, they crawled until reaching another large cavern and tiers of small, barred cells. There, Charcccazee and the other prisoners were incarcerated.

Assigned as a busboy in the Queen's dining rooms, Charcccazee was moved to more comfortable quarters which he shared with three other busboys and where he had his own sleeping cubicle. Among his first assignments was the Royal House's Slobobslob Banquet. He served Slobobslob Stroganoff, Eight-legged Stew, and Slobobslob Chateaubriand, the latter the heads of Hawker and Willie steaming with wine and gravy in a garland of flowers and vegetables.

Charcccazee hated his work: clearing and setting the candlelit tables, changing the pink linen and polishing the long-stemmed goblets and brocaded silverware, or carrying heavy trays on his back. Being a busboy would be difficult enough if he were a boy, but as a cricket it was much worse because instead of hands he had claws, and instead of naturally standing upright he had to rise unnaturally on his hind legs. Glasses, plates, and bottles continually slipped from his grasp, and his boss, a female worker ant, harassed him.

One evening she made him so nervous that a tray full of dinners slid off his back next to the table of Princess Cordelia, the Queen's daughter. The proper and genteel ladies shrieked and moaned.

"You stupid, little cricket," his boss screamed. "What's wrong with you?"

She bashed him with her mandibles.

"Perhaps you would be of better service if we relieved you of your duties and ate you."

Enraged, Charcccazee tossed a glass that just missed the heads of some lady ants.

"Eat me!" he shouted. "I don't care! I can't take this anymore! Eat me and get it over with!"

Two huge soldiers put him into a solitary cell. And thereafter, he worked on toilet patrol.

Soon, Charcccazee became sick and depressed. He refused to work and stopped eating. Better to starve to death than get fat and be eaten. Charcccazee's case was brought to the Queen's divinologist, Sir Dudley Dantley. An ant possessed with unusual powers, he divined Charcccazee to once have been the boy known as "Charles the Bloodletter." Charges were made, and Charcccazee was ordered to stand trial before the Queen at the Hall of Execution.

On the day of his trial, Charcccazee sat alone in his cell. Faced with the possibility of being served on a silver tray like the Slobobslob, he thought about when he was a boy, of his father, mother and Mindy, of how he wished that he had tried harder at piano; of Gino and Kippy and the Tongue's tongue; of Pepperoni and his pizza; of the Professor and his Elizabeth, whom Charcccazee had since learned was sacrificed to the Beastosoreass; of Windy and whether she had made it to the Gorge Ess Ness; and of Bobby whom the ants never found. Never would he see any of them again. His thoughts sped by so fast that it was as if they all blended into one painful recollection.

But the winds of fortune were bringing him better luck. A fateful breeze had blown Windy, his sister seed, upon the very mountain housing the Amazon colony. From a rocky clearing near the mountaintop, she was gazing at a hawk sailing into the lazy clouds that partially obscured the bright sun.

"Hey there, little seed," said a voice.

Stepping out backwards from behind a boulder was Sloppy Bobby, his head twisted around to face her.

"Don't worry, I'm harmless," he said.

Windy stared at Bobby who dwarfed her.

"What do you want?" she asked.

Bobby told her about the battle with the ants and the capture of his rock band.

"I'm looking for a new place to settle down," he said finally. "I love to eat ants, and up here there's one of the largest colonies around."

"Well, I'm really glad you're here," Windy said. "I've been very lonely since I lost my brother. Such a strange little seed. Imagine, he said he used to be a boy."

Before their conversation ended, Bobby and Windy realized that Charlie and Charcccazee were the same young soul. When he revealed Charcccazee's whereabouts to her, she became excited. Not only had the rarefied air told her that the Gorge Ess Ness was near, but Dandelion Lore decreed that before one could enter the realm, they would have to pass a test. Rescuing Charlie, or rather Charcccazee, was such a test, she believed.

Bobby tried to talk her out of it. More likely, he reasoned, it would land her in a salad or cause her to be boiled for tea. Also, she would have to remove her parachute to enter the colony, and this would reduce her chance of reaching the Gorge Ess Ness. She wouldn't listen.

Bobby, who had taken a liking to Windy, decided that despite the dangers he would help her. Fearing that Charcccazee could be eaten at any time, they devised a plan. Windy would be covered with ant guest rove beetle scent and placed by the ant colony entrance. The ants, who couldn't see well, would mistake her for a misplaced egg and take her to the colony hatchery. Bobby, also using the scent, which incidentally had helped him escape during the battle, would enter the colony and try to learn Charcccazee's whereabouts. After freeing Windy, they would rescue him.

The second part of the plan then would go into operation. Using balloons, made from the sap of milkweed plants, Bobby would inflate Windy into a raft. Then they would escape by way of the river.

The final part of the plan was to construct a new, larger parachute that Windy could use after their escape and resume her attempt to reach the Gorge Ess Ness. Bobby decided to construct a parachute before the rescue because he thought it might come in handy. An expert at such things, he obtained thread from a nearby spider and sewed Windy's detached parachute together with parts of the discarded parachutes of daisy, milkweed, and thistle seeds that were strewn along the mountain slopes. He attached it to a flexible pole, which he took from a thistle, and stored extra thread on a spool made out of a twig. He squeezed the parachute, the uninflated balloons, and the thread into his backpack. With Windy resting atop the backpack on his back and facing backward which in Bobby's case was forward, they headed to the ant colony.

Outside the colony entrance Windy waited, while Bobby hid behind a rock. Before long, two ant workers came out, one behind the other, the antennae of the one in the rear touching the abdomen of the one in front. They inspected Windy, and as Bobby had expected, thought she was an egg and hauled her inside.

Through unlit tunnels they took Windy to the central cavern. There, crowds of ants passed while slave bugs wearing collars washed shop windows, cleaned the sidewalks, and took care of the never-ending garbage.

Meanwhile, Bobby floated on a leaf to the Formic River. Suddenly, loudspeakers blared. "Good day, comrades, this is Auntie Everright with a news bulletin. Charles, the Bloodletter, formerly known as a cricket named Charcccazee, who served in the Queen's Dining Room and with the Toilet Patrol, will be sentenced tonight at 7 p.m. in the Hall of Execution. All colonists are welcome to attend. Work hard and devote everything you do to our great colony, comrades. And have yourself a great day."

As Windy sat in the hatchery alongside countless ant eggs, she realized she had to locate Bobby fast. Hearing the splash of water from time to time -- Bobby had told her the Formic River passed directly in front of the Hall of Execution -- she thought that if she could get to the river, she could follow it to the Hall of Execution and find Bobby. But how could she move stuck in the middle of all these eggs?

Windy thought and thought and thought. So hard did she think, it felt like her brain might break. Only after she grew tired and stopped trying did she get an idea. Perhaps if she tickled the eggs around her, it would get the baby ants inside their shells moving. This would cause a chain reaction that could disperse the eggs and free her from the pack. With enough momentum, she could make it to the nearby river.

Windy worried, whistled, wobbled, and wavered; wangled, waggled, wiggled, and wriggled. And egg after egg started to giggle.

"Hee-ha, hoochee-coochee, coochee-coochee-coochee coo," the sound of the eggs echoed.

Soon their hilarity sent them rolling in every direction. Windy moved with the pack, and as it thinned out, she went end over end, her momentum pushing her free. As she rolled along, she directed herself toward the bank from which she had heard the lapping water. Over the edge she went with a splash. Now she had to find Bobby.

By this time, Charcccazee was being led by two great soldiers into the Hall of Execution. It was a colossal, oval structure like a football stadium. Charcccazee felt faint as they marched him into the arena and the crowd twittered hideously. Every seat was filled.

In front of the execution sites Queen Smellifluous awaited, wearing glasses that covered her face. At least twice as long as any other ant, she was also gaunt and feeble looking. Flanking her were a dozen shorter but stout drones.

Behind Smellifluous were the areas of execution: the roasting pit, the bug trap, the toad cage, and towering over them like a skyscraper, the humongous white porcelain toilet. Charcccazee shuddered.

Drums rolled and soldiers marched Charcccazee before Smellifluous. The drums stopped and the arena silenced.

"Dear Subjects," she twittered. "Last week we roasted the Slobobslob. Now, before us, is sausage from the same celebration, Charles, the Bloodletter."

There was hooting and jeering.

"The time has come for his execution."

The commotion from the crowd grew louder.

"Charles, the Bloodletter," she said, looking sternly at Charcccazee, her eyes magnified by her glasses. "This tribunal has no other recourse but to find you guilty. Guilty for your mindless slaughter of countless, innocent ants. Guilty for being a bad, bad little boy."

Smellifluous smiled and there was uproarious approval.

"It is only for the Grand Drones to decide the method of execution," she said. "Among their choices are death by barbecue, death by poison, death by being thrown to the toads, and the sentence I strongly recommend, death by flushing down the toilet!"

The applause was accompanied by howling. Charcccazee shivered as the Drones huddled and twittered. Finally, they faced the Queen. The foreman whispered to her, and she smiled again.

"Charles, the Bloodletter," she said, "I am so pleased to announce that this court has decided that on this very day, within the next minute, you will be flushed down the toilet, ending your days of bloodletting and terror."

Charcccazee fainted.

As they revived Charcccazee with smelling salts, Windy was in sight of the Hall of Execution. She could hear the din of the crowd. If only she could find Bobby. Little did she realize that Bobby was approaching from the opposite direction.

"Bobby," she said, as she caught sight of him.

"Shhh," Bobby said. "Do as I say."

He took out his balloons and started blowing them up and deflating them into the central crevice in Windy's shell. One after another, he blew them up at a furious pace and deflated them into Windy, inflating her. Soon, she was light and soft, and made a sizeable raft. Bobby crawled atop her. He took the makeshift parachute out of his backpack. He attached its thistle pole with his thread and hoisted up the parachute, also fastening the parachute to Windy. Then, as fast as he could, he blew up more balloons and let them float up under the parachute's canopy.

By this time, Charcccazee was moving up the ramp to the toilet seat, trudging just ahead of the executioner, a huge ant who shoved him forward with his massive mandibles. Stepping upon the smooth, wide, black seat, he looked at his reflection in the water, which looked so clear and clean. His antennae shook, his wing covers jingled, his heart felt about to leap out. Ohh, if only he had learned to swim, if only he hadn't gotten into a fight with his father.

Meanwhile, enough balloons had been blown up to move Windy's makeshift parachute above the river. Bobby now began blowing up one after the other and deflating them, sending blasts of air up under the parachute, making it rise higher. Up and up they went until they were over the arena's walls.

As the executioner placed the blindfold over Charcccazee's eyes, Bobby and Windy coasted over the stadium down toward the great toilet. The crowd, which had turned silent, gasped at the sight of the parachute. Bobby, pulling on the threads that fastened the parachute to Windy, directed it towards the toilet seat. The Queen froze with shock. She shouted to the executioner.

"Now, sir! Now!"

Just as Bobby and Windy landed on the toilet seat, the
executioner knocked Charcccazee off the edge. It was a great
fall into the water, and though Charcccazee had heard the noise
made by his friends' landing, he hadn't seen them. He held his
breath as he plunged in. Helplessly he churned his legs and

antennae, getting water in his mouth, throat, and lungs. He gasped for air but kept going under.

Above, on the toilet seat, Bobby used his jaws to bash the executioner on the head. This dazed the ant and allowed Windy to roll off the seat and into the bowl. Bobby tried to follow, but several ant soldiers came charging up the ramp and grasped him with their mandibles. As they grappled, the executioner flushed the toilet.

Water rushed down into the bowl and caused whirlpools. Everything bubbled, whirled, fizzed, swooshed. Charcccazee was sucked down farther. But Windy was right behind him. The pressure whooshed them through the toilet hole, then the current slowed. Windy coasted under Charcccazee and rose to the surface. He coughed and coughed as his head went above the water. He was only barely conscious yet could feel something under him.

"Are you all right, Charlie, are you all right?" Windy shouted.

Charcccazee puffed air and coughed; he recognized her voice.

"Windy," he took a breath. "Windy."

"Charlie!"

He sucked harder.

"Windy," he breathed. "It's really you?"

"Yes, Charlie," she said. "It's me."

"But," he puffed, "but where did you come from, and how did you get so fat?"

"I think it's a miracle, Charlie. Everything's a miracle. Do you realize where we are?"

Windy assured him that they were on the brink of the Gorge Ess Ness. She didn't realize that the current was taking them in the opposite direction. As she explained how she had met Bobby, how he had inflated her, and how they rescued him, the pipe widened and putrid odors intensified. Soon they had joined a herd of floating filth. Charcccazee had never been in such a disgusting place.

Chapter Fifteen
Sweetly Chirping

Being reunited with Windy made Charcccazee almost as happy as if he were a boy again. Even the floating filth didn't bother him. Coasting through larger pipes that led to a wide tunnel, they reached an opening that emptied outside into a river the color of regular coffee. Floating in it were Big Ben hamburger containers from Benedict Arnold's, dented beer cans, empty cigarette packs, gum wrappers, a Pump It Up sneaker, a tire, and a dead fish with its bloodshot eye staring up vacantly. What a stench! Yet the birds continued to sing.

"See, see, see. Where, where. Look at me."

"Poor, Poor. Sam, Sam. Pea-body."

"Come, come, come out, come out, wherever you are."

"Hey, hey, Ellen — hee-yah. Hey, hey, Ellen — hee-yah."

Their words were not clear, but their soft tremolos were melodious. Then a war cry shrilled. A massive red bird blazed over Charcccazee and Windy. The crest atop its head stood on end as it snatched them with its black bearded beak. As the bird flew above the trees, Charcccazee squirmed and screamed.

"What is this bird going to do to us, Windy?"

"Let's not think about it, Charlie."

"But is it going to eat us?"

"Charlie, stop it."

Charcccazee began crying.

"Calm down, Charlie. He hasn't eaten us yet. Who knows, we might still get away."

They came to a city, and flew over crisscrossing streets, roofs with TV satellite dishes and antennas, and yards with clotheslines. Charcccazee felt Windy, who was deflating, slipping away. Finally, she fell from the bird's grip as they passed over a church steeple, dropping like a bomb.

"Charlie!" she cried.

Once again, he was separated from his sister seed and soon she was out of sight. Poor Charcccazee. He was terrified. The bird flew into a park and glided to a maple tree. Behind its thick foliage, the bird shook its wings and landed on a nest. It dropped Charcccazee inside. At once a gray bird struck, shearing off Charcccazee's head. It was like the time he was with the Tongue and the giant rat bolted after him. A shock and a screech. This time, though, as the bird swallowed him, it seemed more real, more like it was actually happening.

Down a moist, dark passageway leading through several caverns with grunts, groans, and fizzes he slid. Everything churned and fluids sprayed like hot showers. Down he continued, as if moving on a slide until he mashed into a wall of smelly paste. A great rumbling followed, and Charcccazee felt as if absorbed into something else.

He had no idea how long he remained like this. It could've been days or weeks but seemed only minutes before the first light peeked through. No longer was he a cricket but something breaking through to the outside. He heard tweedling and eyed the most vividly colored day he'd ever seen.

Two huge birds were perched on the wall of a nest, one fiery red, the other pale gray with patches of red on its beak, crest, and wings. Also, next to him were two moist, furry, brown baby birds.

"We-oo, we-oo, we-oo," the grayish bird sang. "I am your mama, my little darling daughter, Cha-la-la. These are your brothers, Cha-la-lee and Cha-la-la ha-ha."

Daughter? This was something very different indeed. But it wasn't just that he wasn't himself anymore. He was now a she—Cha-la-la, a baby chick.

"Cha-la-lee, Cha-la-la, Cha-la-lee, Cha-la-la-ha-ha-ha, la-ha-ha-ha," her mother sang. "Time to eat your din-din, so open up your beaks."

As if on instinct, Cha-la-la and her brothers answered.

"Feed me, feed me, feed me."

"We-oo, we-oo, we-willlll," their mother crooned.

Their parents fed them seed granola and the choicest parts of locusts, cicadas, beetles, moths, caterpillars, and crickets. Everything tasted as good as a Geronimo's pizza or a Big Ben with lettuce, pickles, onions, cheese and special sauce on a sesame seed bun. Then a hideous thought occurred. Cha-la-la had been both a seed and a bug, and now she was eating seeds and bugs. Who knows but she might be eating a relative of the Professor or heaven forbid even Windy herself! There was no way to tell because now that she was a bird, every seed or bug looked pretty much the same. Yet she just didn't seem to stop being hungry. Even as a boy, she had never eaten so much or so well.

For birds, time blurs by in dazzling colors, especially rich shades of yellow, orange, and red, and their little hearts beat with a frenzy that makes their bodies warmer than most other creatures. Weeks to them seem as if only a day. And throughout it all, Cha-la-la did little but eat, sleep, and learn to sing.

Finally, it was time to leave the nest. Her brothers had long since left and her parents, now out gathering food, were ready to leave. She hopped out onto the tree branches and puffed her thick gray feathers that had grown in place of the brown baby fluff.

"Goodbye, Kieran," she said to her maple tree.

"Be careful, Cha-la-la," he said in his deep voice.

She shook her wings and puffed her breast. Something told her she was ready to fly. She moved up the branch until the leaves had thinned and there was enough room to jump. Rocking back and forth, she hopped off the branch. Her heart raced as she dropped down. Struggling like someone learning to swim, she furiously flapped her wings. Somehow she reached another branch.

She was shaking. Though she had flown only a short distance, it was a start. She was ready to try again. She imagined herself flying and jumped into the air. Her wings felt stronger, more synchronized. Like someone at the end of a great broad jump, she dropped onto the branch of a nearby tree.

She felt ready to really fly now. Closing her eyes, she flapped her wings. Up she rose, up and up until she was above the trees. She coasted over Kieran.

"God love ya, Cha-la-la!" he called.

She looked down at Kieran who waved his leaves in the breeze.

"When ya grow up, girl, remember your big old honey tree."

Kieran was referring to the honeybees who had a nest in his branches and who always delivered bit-o-honeys to her parents free of charge.

"I will, I will, Kieran. I promise I will."

After several more jaunts with rests in between, Cha-la-la rocketed above, marveling at the sky and the clouds, and the way they blended into the earth at the edge of the horizon. Up she soared, her wings working like the legs of a distance runner. Finally, she was up so high she was able to rest her wings against the soft air. As she glided, everything felt free and easy. She became entranced by the colors that made up the earth, the changing shapes of the clouds, the infinite blues of the sky, and the reflections in the ponds, lakes, and rivers below.

Across vast spaces she flew, stopping only to eat and sleep. For days she wandered, though it was hard to tell how long, until she came upon a skyline of buildings. She recognized them. It was Windy City, where Uncle Vince and Cousin Roger lived.

Above them all was the Epic Proportions Building, once again the world's tallest, crowned by a structure that looked like a three-stage rocket. It had been the world's tallest for many years until several taller buildings went up. Then, just recently, a second bullet-shaped structure was built atop the original one, making it the world's tallest again.

Cha-la-la looked down at all the stone buildings, appearing like so many squares, rectangles, circles, and triangles. How dirty and filthy they seemed in comparison to the countryside. She began to feel lonely. The only birds she saw were pigeons, sparrows, crows, and sea gulls, all with colors as drab as the city. She didn't want to stay here.

Cha-la-la left as fast as she could. For hours she journeyed, stopping only to eat some berries and a juicy beetle. Finally, she came to an area similar to where she was born. She wondered if she might see her parents. But that was unlikely. Cardinals choose new mates each year and aren't interested in seeing their former children.

Next to a lonely pond surrounded by several trees, she splashed herself with water. She watched the surface clear and reveal her image. Her face was ivory white and adorned by a bright red beak and her crest was gray with streaks of red. A pretty girl she was, for sure.

Suddenly, she heard a song begin. How wonderful, she thought. Never had she imagined singing like this. She flew up from the pond onto a branch in the tree closer to the singing and spotted the singer. What a beautiful coat he had, as red as Santa Claus's, with a black beard around his beak. He didn't look at her but continued singing.

For some time this went on: she moving closer though never within speaking distance; he singing his heart out, weaving variations of his song. Then, something made her break into song.

"Phoooh-oooooh . . . Phoooh-oooooh . . . Phooh-oooooh . . ."

In the middle of her singing, the male landed on her branch. He was a bit larger and perhaps older.

"Your singing's beautiful," he said. "Have you ever sung to a boy before?"

Cha-la-la felt shy. She didn't know what to say.

"Would you build me a nest and lay the eggs from which our children will hatch?" he asked.

He looked into her dark eyes and something drew them to each other. He told her his name was Roger and she told him hers. He sang to her with all his heart. Cha-la-la felt the sound ruffle her crest and move down her neck and back.

His voice grew louder and more harmonious, but a deeper and more powerful voice intruded.

Behind them a male Cardinal, older and much larger than Roger, puffed his breast. He had a tall red crest shaped like a Bishop's crown. Roger confronted him.

"Get out, get out, you hear what I say," Roger screeched. "If you don't get out, I'm gonna go out there and fling you out."

The older bird warbled a sound like laughter.

"Don't be foolish, young bird," he said. "Go find yourself another territory and another mate. This one is mine."

"Fooey to you, fooey to you, fooey to you!" Roger responded.

"Oh yeah, buddy!" the older bird cried and leaped from his branch.

In an instant the older bird was upon Roger and knocked him off his perch. Roger caught his balance, his wings treading the air. But the bigger bird dove at him again, knocking him all the way to the ground. Almost as soon as Roger landed, the bird dive bombed into him.

Cha-la-la watched in shock. Roger's feathers flew as the big bird held him down and thrashed him with his tail. She had to do something. Flying off her perch, she bounded into the older bird. Instead of knocking him off Roger, she bounced off the bird onto the ground. Dazed, she passed out.

When she awoke, she ached all over, but far worse was the sight of Roger's rigid body.

Chapter Sixteen
Remembrance of a Song Past

Roger's death made Cha-la-la feel as if she were in some foggy place separated from everything. She felt exhausted and that night perched in one of the forest's highest and loneliest trees. But every time she dozed off, she was awakened by a nightmare of Roger overhead, his wings aflurry, trying to sing yet unable. Finally, by morning she fell asleep.

When she awoke that afternoon, she had slipped into an even deeper fog. She had forgotten everything that had come before in her life. Even more puzzling were the hundreds of male suitors surrounding her and singing to win her love, with even more filling up the forest. It was like what a celebrity must feel in the midst of an audience. Louder and louder the birds became, blending like a chorus, making their individual songs indecipherable.

Cha-la-la fled. Fortunately, only a few birds followed and those soon gave up the chase. She continued flying, however, as fast and far as she could. Maybe a hundred miles she went before landing on a tree among a swatch of trees near a pond in the hilltops. She was hungry but couldn't eat. Instead, she started crying. Not loud, hysterical cries but gentle sobs that touched the heart of a fluttering bug with a

long, neede thin tail, large transparent wings, and a black head and vest.

"Don't cry, my dear. Everything'll be all right," the bug said, very grandmotherly.

Cha-la-la stopped crying.

"Who are you?" she asked.

"My name's Mary. I'm a mayfly."

"Do you live here?" Cha-la-la asked.

"Only for today. You see, after living for many years in the water, I underwent a metamorphosis. This morning I left my pond to lay my eggs. In fact, I had just laid them when I heard you crying."

"Shouldn't you get back to them?" Cha-la-la asked.

Mary laughed.

"My eggs don't need me now. They'll hatch all by themselves. No, I'm ready to die." "Die?"

"Yes, life lasts but a day for a mayfly."

Cha-la-la shook her head in sympathy.

"And what is your name?" Mary asked.

"Cha-la-la."

"I like that name," Mary said and smiled. "Why were you crying, Cha-la-la?"

"Because something awful happened to me, but I can't remember what it was. All I know is that I've been flying a long time and I'm hungry."

"Ohh, I'm so sorry, my dear," Mary said. "Don't worry, Cha-la-la. Someday everything'll come back to you, as well as memories of all the lives you've lived before."

"What lives?"

"Our past lives. We all have past lives and we all come back and live again. When I die today, it won't be the end of me, not for long. I'll come back as something else. Oh, I've lived some pretty exciting lives before this one."

"Really?"

"Indeed. One time I was a woman who had a husband who was a famous poet, and I was a writer too. I wrote a fantastic book about a man who creates a monster and brings him to life. They often performed it on stage during my life. Later, after I died, they made a whole series of movies based on it. And to this very day people still read my book. Perhaps in this life or in a past life, you read it."

"I don't remember," Cha-la-la said.

"That's alright," Mary said. "But one thing I am sure of is that you have lived another life. You know, Cha-la-la, you look awful thin. You should eat something."

"I can't eat, Mary. I don't feel well."

"But you've got to eat, Cha-la-la. Birds can't live long without food, especially if you've been flying for a long time."

Mary fluttered her wings.

"I'm about ready to die, Cha-la-la. If you want, you can eat me. I promise I'll make a delicious supper."

"I couldn't eat you, Mary."

"Why not?"

"Because. Because you're my friend."

"That's all the more reason to eat me. Then I'll become a part of you. Wouldn't that be nice?"

Mary's wings quivered, her antennae drooped, and her breathing quickened. Her black face turned gray and her wings stopped moving. She looked up at Cha-la-la with longing.

"Please, Cha-la-la. Please, eat me. Please."

Mary closed her eyes, sighed, and slumped on the branch.

"Mary," Cha-la-la cried. "Mary! Are you all right, are you all right?"

Mary never answered. Cha-la-la didn't know what to do. But over and over in her mind, she could hear Mary's dying request: `Please, Cha-la-la. Please, eat me. Please.'

Finally, and very quickly, Cha-la-la ate her. She tried not to notice the taste but once she finished she felt better. Her stomach was full again and she wondered whether she had lived other lives like Mary said. Then a deep voice called to her.

"Whooooo. Whooooo. Whooooo goes there?"

Cha-la-la looked across the way to a massive oak tree and saw an owl wearing large, horn rimmed glasses perched on a branch.

"I say whooooo is it that has come to visit my glen?" the owl asked.

Cha-la-la grew frightened.

"Come. Come over to my tree," the owl said. "I am not one whooooo is bent on violence."

Cha-la-la jumped over to a branch below the owl. Though the owl was bigger, he wasn't as big as most owls and rather gaunt as well, his bones sticking out from under his feathers. He was an old owl, and his most striking feature was his head, which looked much bigger than the rest of his body.

"You look like one whooooo might be lost," the owl said. "Perhaps I can assist yooooou?"

"I'm not sure," Cha-la-la said. "I've forgotten everything and I don't know what to do."

"Well, then, you've come to the right place. Here birds whooooo seek the riches of the spirit come to find themselves."

"What spirit?"

"The Great Spirit. Whooooo we cannot see nor touch but know is there. And believe me, if you seek to find not merely your past but its meaning, you shall find it here."

"I will?"

"Of course. I have devoted my life to this search. Unlike others whooooo fly off on great ordeals around the earth, I am content staying here. Often those whooooo are off on great quests to find what or whooooom they think they are trying to find, miss what or whooooo is before their very eyes. But here in my glen I miss nothing. I read, relax, and listen tooooo everything around me. And at night I, whooooo am one with the Great Spirit, sing the great song that answers our every want. What more could yooooou or anyone need?"

The owl coughed.

"Excuse me," the owl said. "I've got a noxious cold that doesn't seem to want to go away. Sometimes one hasn't the time for anything but to deal with such unpleasantries. But I shouldn't trouble yooooou with my problems. Tell me, what is your name?"

Cha-la-la replied, and the owl told her he was Peter, but also known as the Owlkapellmeister.

"Come, Cha-la-la. Come into my nest and rest awhile. You can stay the night if you wish."

She followed him as he tottered into a hollowed-out portion of the tree, which formerly had been the home of a red-headed woodpecker and which he had expanded and improved upon. The living room, with a small organ, cot, and rocking chair, overflowed with books.

"Do you mind if I play some music?" Peter asked.

Cha-la-la had no objection, for somehow she realized that music had become part of her life. After Peter cranked up his organ, he wrapped himself in a thick blanket, slumped into his rocking chair and closed his eyes. The music's melody was familiar. Cha-la-la could not remember where she had heard it, but did remember being told it was the song of the Delius.

This time, though, instead of one bird singing, a rich chorus of chords filled the air. In his surprisingly tuneful voice, Peter began quietly dee-dah dumming along. When it ended, he stopped and opened his eyes.

"Perhaps you have heard this song before? I know it's a modest work but it's my personal favorite."

"It's the song of the Delius, isn't it?" Cha-la-la asked.

"Why, yes," Peter said. "So, you have heard it. Well, well, I am quite surprised. I did not expect to meet someone who knew of my music."

"Your music?"

"Yes, I must confess, it is I whoooo am the Delius. Peter Frederick Delius, owlkapellmeister, composer, conductor, dramaturge, poet, and music critic. I have been all of these. And now I have come to this glen to take my place with the Great Spirit."

That night after listening to more of Peter's music, Cha-la-la began to recall her past in a rush of memory from the time she was Charles until the death of Roger. She told Peter everything. The old owl, who had lived a long life and experienced great suffering himself, was not surprised. He explained that life is full of surprises. Even the Great Spirit had no way of knowing what would happen next.

Peter had thought much about the uncertainty of life and had written an opera which offered a solution to this problem called "Be with Ye Brethren." It suggested that all creatures be gentle with one another because everyone is part of everything else. No one or thing ever ends, Peter believed -- they simply continue in that which follows. And Peter talked for hours. Only when the morning sun peeked over the hills did he doze off.

Chapter Seventeen

Happiness is Yappiness

Peter was still sleeping when Cha-la-la left the next morning. She didn't want to wake the sick, old owl. Instead, she left a sprig of evergreen, signifying thank you, and slipped out quietly. His wisdom had put her at ease.

She flew out of the glen into the blue-lake sky feeling rejuvenated. After flying over several valleys and stretches of woodland, she came to a lake. She gathered berries and perched in a tree along the shore.

Though there was no sign of a storm, thunder flapped in the distance and grew louder. Peering out over the hills, she saw a shimmering swirl of blue approaching. It looked like a row of huge wheels rolling along. The thunder turned into a wordless chorus, and Cha-la-la could see that the swirls were actually a great flock of birds. As they filled the sky and descended in thick columns their poignant song resonated across the horizon.

Down they swung into the trees, including the one where Cha-la-la perched. The trees shook and bent as the birds loaded up their branches. Soon Cha-la-la was surrounded. Most of the birds resembled graceful pigeons with long tails and plumage the color of bluebirds, but also among them were two types of larger birds. One, about twice the size of the pigeons, had webbed feet, long black bills, and black and white plumage; the other, more turkey like and of a light to charcoal gray coloring, had a bulging belly and a greenish black hooked beak that gave it a sinister expression.

One of the latter landed on Cha-la-la's branch.

Ponderously, it shuffled closer to her.

"You yon't mind, yewe you young yady," the bird asked in a high voice, then gasped for air, "if I stop and rest here?"

Cha-la-la's beak dropped open in amazement. The bird took another deep breath.

"I'll try yew speak yore slowly. Yaey I rest here awhile?"

"Sure," Cha-la-la said.

"You see," said the bird, "we are the Yoyos, and we speak a yanguage yalled Yappiness. We yake everything yappy, that is, we substitute y's for the yonsonants at the beginning of yords which are yollowed by a's and o's except when they begin with a yowel or youble yonsonant. Of

yourse, there are yomm exceptions and yomm yariations in spelling."

"Oh," said Cha-la-la.

"Yon't yorry, you'll get used yew it."

Getting used to the language of Yappiness wasn't easy, but Cha-la-la managed. The Yoyo, whose name was Yolanda, explained that the Yoyos had given up their old lives to follow the teachings of the first Yoyo, a pigeon who had escaped from a zoo after being enlightened. This bird became known as the Yaster. Among the truths which the Yaster came to understand was that all birds who could not fly were doomed to extinction. With the degradation of the environment, even those who could fly had become threatened because it was unlikely that any birds could survive in the Underground World that the animal kingdom was preparing. So, the spiritual quest the Yaster had started had become even more important.

The duck-like birds, who had called themselves Quawks, and those like Yolanda, who had been known as the Yozzers, were among the first to lose the power of flight. Naturally, they were attracted to the teachings of the Yaster and they joined the Yoyos to learn how to fly again.

"We invite all birds yew yoin us on our yourney, Cha-ya-ya," Yolanda said.

"Where are you going?" asked Cha-la-la.

"The Bermuda Triangle."

"Where's that?"

"In the Atlantic Ocean, where all yorts of mysterious and yarvelous things yappen. But the yost yarvelous yappening of all is the yole in the sky that opens to where the Great White Yooneys fly."

"And who are the Yooneys?"

"The perfect and all-knowing birds who regulate creation. It is said that once yommone sees them, they will never be unyappy again."

"Have you seen them?"

"Oh yoh. Once you see them, you will stay with them yorever."

Cha-la-la thought for a moment.

"But if everyone who sees them stays with them, then who comes back to tell you that they're really there?"

"Because, if they weren't there, there yould be yoh one yew regulate the heavens. And if the heavens weren't regulated, then yoh yappiness yood exist, and everyone knows that is yot yo."

Cha-la-la couldn't argue with that.

"Where are you headed, Cha-ya-ya?" Yolanda asked.

"I don't know. Something very bad happened to me and I need time to think."

"Why yon't you yoin us?"

"I don't know," Cha-la-la said. "Do you think seeing the Yooneys will help me?"

"Believe me, Cha-ya-ya, if you yome with us, you will find your answers. Yow, I will yot yache yoh yor an answer. Besides, in our yanguage there is yoh such yord as yoh. There is only yes—yes-yes-yes. Yaye yes, Cha ya-ya."

Cha-la-la had nowhere else to go and thought that if the Triangle was a place where fantastic things happened, then maybe this was where she should go. The next day she took off with the flock. All day and night they flew until they reached a tropical island.

After resting in a grove of palm trees, they glided down to the beach. Squatting together on the smooth white sand, they gathered around a pigeon, who led them in the practice of yoga.

"Everyone, close your eyes," the bird said softly. "Keep your yack straight. Breathe easily. Yow, let's inhale and chant yohm."

Cha-la-la looked around and saw that the other birds had closed their eyes and were inhaling until their bellies were swollen.

"Yohhhhhhhhh-mmmmmmmmmmmmmmmm," they chanted in harmony.

When the last sounds faded, the leader resumed the exercise. It involved deep breathing and concentration, and Cha-la-la found the routine monotonous and difficult. However, the breathing exercises were only the beginning. They were followed by a series of positions that alternately tensed and relaxed the body. They felt strange to Cha-la-la. Not really uncomfortable but awkward. Then they entered the period for deep relaxation when they lay back and let their body go limp. At a point she was not aware of, a peacefulness washed over her and caused her to fall asleep. Gently, Yolanda woke her.

"Cha-ya-ya," she said, "it's time yew yather flowers yor the nightly offering."

Cha-la-la rubbed her eyes.

"But I'm hungry. Can't we eat something first?"

"Oh yoh. Yewyay you must yast. One yay each week we eat yothing."

"All day?"

Yolanda laughed.

"One yay is yothing. Before you yan yoe see the Yooneys you must yast yor three yays."

"But why? What's the purpose?

"Yew must cleanse your yody of impurities. But yore important, it yakes you realize that yew be yappy, you must yot be enslaved by your cravings for the things of this yorld. You may yot understand this yow, but you will yommyay. It's merely a yatter of mind over yatter."

The activities kept Cha-la-la's mind off food. But, later, she thought about anchovyburgers, french fried berries, taco nuts, and chocolate seeds. Only the willpower of the group enabled her to resist.

That evening, the Yoyos offered up the perfume of the flowers they had gathered for a great bonfire. It created the most wonderful incense and they chanted in a language even stranger than yappiness. This led into extended chanting of yohm, and relaxed Cha-la-la so that she easily fell asleep.

Next morning, after a breakfast of berries, the flock flew into a strawberry sunrise full of chiffon clouds. This sweet sight and the rhythm of their wings brought her tranquility. It was one of those moments in life when everything was bliss.

But perfection never lasts long. Moving swiftly from the south was a vulture-shaped mass of black clouds. Coming across the storm's path they saw a flock of tiny hummingbirds. The hummingbirds appeared to be moving in slow motion, and the storm was about to engulf them. The Yoyos quickly flew up to escape. They watched helplessly as the storm churned into the hummingbirds, heaving them in various directions into the sea.

Later, after the storm, the Yoyos descended and found the hummingbirds' lifeless bodies tossing in the waves. Cha-la-la started to cry. Yolanda, however, remained calm.

"Living things are only temporary, Cha-ya-ya," Yolanda said. "There is yoh unchanging, everlasting thing. Because of this we suffer, but it is also because of this that we yan be yappy. We know that yommyay we will never yav yew suffer again."

In the following days, Cha-la-la practiced yoga, meditation, and fasting. She strove to conform to the commandments of the Yoyos: Birds yewe yot live by seeds alone; those who give, shall receive; those who are meek will be strong; and those who need yoh one, will never be yonely. She also learned new flying techniques, like catching a ride from heat lifting off the ground.

Gradually, her endurance grew. She forgot about building a nest and raising a family. Mind over yatter, Yolanda constantly reminded her, is the yaye to the Yooneys. And each day of meditation seemed to bring her to new heights when the eternal moment engulfed her, and each moment seemed to last longer though the days rushed by. Now Cha-la-la knew what it meant to be holy, or rather yoly.

Finally, one evening when the crickets were singing and the stars so clear they made one blink, the flock was ready to attempt their flight to the Yooneys. The Keeper of the Yong prepared his instruments.

"Yawtch the breath," the meditation leader said. "Let yoe of all negative thoughts. Witness the other thoughts and let them yass. Let yoe of everything. Open your eyes and yocus on the sky. Imagine a star shooting across. Imagine it growing into a yomet. A yomet yizzing across the sky. Yow keep yoncentrating as we chant yohm."

The Keeper of the Yong readied. As the flock let out an ultimate yohm, he struck his mighty yong which reverberated along with the flock.

"YOHHHHHHHHMMMM!"

At that moment, a great tail of light lit across the starry horizon. The flock rose from their squatting positions. Soft tissues of sound passed through and a puff of air glided off the sea. It took them up like hot air balloons. Thousands of feet they rose until they were so high they felt they could touch the stars. Cha-la-la felt as if she had left her body as she glided in the thick, resplendent sigh-lence . . .

"Yowow-yowwww," came a distant cry. "Yowow-yowwww! Yowow-yowwww!"

The cries grew louder.

"Yowow-yowwww! Yowow-yowwww! Yowow-yowwww!"

The flock gazed overheard. They saw the night sky open.

"Yowow-yowwww! Yowow-yowwww! Yowow-yowwww!"

The cries were deafening now.

"YOWOW-YOWWWW! YOWOW-YOWWWW! YOWOW-YOWWWW!"

Yolanda gazed at Cha-la-la and began shouting something, and though she couldn't hear her, it looked like she was saying Yooneys. The Yoyos flew toward the opening. It was much farther than it appeared. There was less air to breathe. It became colder and darker. Everyone started gasping and Cha-la-la found that most of the others were slipping behind. She was high enough now to see something, something blinding white passing over.

"YOWOW OOOOH! YOWOW OOOOH! YOWOW OOOOH! YOWOW OOOOH! YOWOW OOOOH!"

Cha-la-la struggled but could go no higher. The harder she flapped her wings, the weaker she became. She started to lose control and fall. Fortunately, the thicker air below slowed her. Barely flapping her wings, she no longer saw the ocean but a brilliant network of lights. A ghostly wind slinked through. Shivering, she lost control again and plummeted towards the crisscrossed lights. They blinded her as she closed in on the skyscrapers. It reminded her of the lighthouse eyes of Dennis, the Preying Menace. She bounced against the side of a building and was deflected into another. Her skull cracked. The pain was unbearable. Completely helpless, she crashed with a thud to the pavement in an alley.

Cha-la-la was barely alive, and hurrying down with lilacs was Yolanda. She stood over Cha-la-la.

"Cha-ya-ya, Cha-ya-ya."

Cha-la-la blinked her eyes.

"Cha-ya-ya," Yolanda cried. "Cha-ya-ya, you yav yone it, you yav seen the Great White Yooneys."

Cha-la-la smiled faintly.

"The Yooneys dropped us these lilacs," said Yolanda. "Smell them, Cha-ya-ya."

Cha-la-la sniffed but could barely smell their perfume.

"It's all right, Cha-ya-ya. It's all right. Everything is, Cha-ya-ya. Everything is."

Cha-la-la gave one last weak smile and closed her eyes.

Chapter Eighteen
The Spirit of the Flesh

Cha-la-la's spirit left her body and merged with the lilacs. She wished the sobbing Yolanda could understand, but Cha-la-la could only roll with the gentle drafts.

Yolanda wrapped the lilacs around the body and chanted over it. Someone was coming, so she looked at Cha-la la's body one last time and flew away.

A large black woman with a shopping bag approached. A scarf swaddled around her forehead, a baggy sweatshirt hung nearly to her knees, and high-top sneakers met the cuffs of her jeans. She stopped when she came to Cha-la-la's body and squatted down. Noticing the lilacs around the body, her mouth opened and her eyes bulged. She put the body in the palm of her hand. Cha-la-la felt a twinge, for she was still connected to her body. The lady brought the body closer to her face.

"Poor dead birdie," she said.

With her free hand, she reached into her shopping bag, and took out a small plastic baggy. Into it she slid the body and the lilacs. After putting the baggy into her bag, she walked out of the alley.

Everywhere people hurried, laughed, shouted; automobiles squealed; horns blared; exhaust settled. Anything could happen in a city: maniacs with guns, rats bigger than cats, mad dogs, fires, car crashes, sirens! The woman stood at an intersection as a police car wheeled past.

Through the crowd the woman walked until she reached a park on the edge of town. Spacious, well lit, and patrolled by the police, it was one of her favorite haunts. She buried the body behind a park bench and stuck the lilac branch into the dirt over the grave.

That night roots sprouted from the branch and burrowed into the soil. As it grew colder, they rested. But when the night departed and the sun climbed the looming skyscrapers, the roots stirred again. Their excitement grew and they stiffened in the soil as shoots mushroomed out of the earth like the famous beanstalk, climbing up and up into a tree-sized bush of lilacs. They were exhaling great breaths of pink perfume, which Cha-la-la had become. How free to be something so ethereal and wonderful, unencumbered by physical limitations. It was as her spirit was savoring these fragrant moments that along came a squirrel-sized rodent with a large head, big brown eyes, and a short dark tail.

"Only mek beelif, I loaf jew," he sang in his Mexican accent. "Only mek beelif, dat jew loaf me. Ay, to find, peace of mine, een pretendeeng. Couldn't jew, couldn't I, couldn't we?"

He smelled the lilacs and stopped. Hopping to the bush, he took in a deeper whiff, and once again the spirit of Charles, had taken another form. The rodent felt different too. He wasn't sure why, but he felt like he had entered a crossroads and had become more than just the prairie dog named Tontoriso Jimejonez, pronounced "Dondoritho He-mayonnaise."

It seemed so long since Tonto, as everyone called him, had relaxed in the cozy burrows of his home dogtown and gazed upon its tan prairies. He had crossed so many superhighways, bridges, and forested mountains that they all looked the same. But he was determined to reach his destination. With things getting crowded in his home dogtown, he had decided to try his luck with the circus.

Since a young dog, Tonto had heard stories about the Capellini Circus. And like his uncle before him, he was breaking the prairie dog's oldest commandment: "Thou shalt live in the prairie, and the prairie only."

However, the disappearance of the prairie and the deadly poisons spreading through the dogtowns had made it necessary for daring dogs like him to break the commandment and come east. His late uncle had worked for a circus in the East and always said that if Tonto wanted to join the circus, that if he mentioned that he was his nephew, all the circuses would know of him and would hire Tonto and teach him how to be a performer. Now he was going to do just that.

According to his directions, he had to find the brook that ran through this very park and follow it to the river. The circus was visiting a site beneath a human amusement park, a short distance from a cluster of abandoned factory buildings that sat along the river.

When he arrived, he scanned the park and sniffed the ground. Under lilacs and the hint of dandelion, was a berry ambrosia. He followed it toward a gully covered with shrubs and weeds. It led to a patch of blueberries. He picked the juicy clusters and sucked them. Mmm. Then he heard the trickle of water. He noticed that under thick grass and weeds was a stream. He hopped down and saw his reflection in the greenish pool. But just as he was about to take a dip, a voice called.

"Hey, good buddy, I wouldn't do that."

Tonto turned and saw a large, powerfully built raccoon with a wooden hind leg and a  patch over his eye. Tonto froze.

"No, pliss, Senor Raccoon," he said, "pliss do not eat me."

"Don't worry, good buddy," the raccoon said and held up his paw. "I won't hurt ya. I'm a vegetarian."

The raccoon limped toward Tonto, who moved back.

"Just warnin' ya about the water, is all. It's polluted."

Tonto's fear eased. He remembered hearing the word polluted before but couldn't place where.

"Pah looted?"

"It ain't good for ya, buddy."

"How jew know dis?" Tonto asked.

"I seen the raw sewage coming right out of the pipes myself. You must be new here. I never seen a squirrel like you."

"Si, I what dey call a barkeeng dog or prairie dog. We comb from dee Midwest. I comb here to yoin dee circus, dee Capellini Circus. Jew know eet?"

"Sure, it's not too far from here. In fact, that's where I'm headed myself, to audition for Ringmaster. Did you know they've relocated underground?"

"Arrima! No!"

"You haven't heard about the new Underground World?" Ricky asked.

"No," Tonto said.

"The world's burrowing animals are creating a great underground network where we can make our new home as a refuge from the changing climate."

"Ah, we no hear dat on dee prairie. Ees really that bad?"

"I'm afraid so," Ratchett said, then changed the subject. "What you fixing to be?"

"Ay, any yob is okay with me. My uncle, he was a clown for Capellini. He say eef I tell dem I hees nephew, dey fine me a yob."

"If they don't find ya something, my aunt'll help ya. She makes the costumes there. By the way," the raccoon extended his paw, "my name's Ricky, Ricky Ratchett."

"I am Dondo," Tonto said. "Dondo Jimezjones."

They followed the stream for a few miles to the river, passing a section of abandoned factory buildings with broken windows. Over rocks at the riverbank they hopped past an old canal that led to a wooded area. This headed away from the river. Up through the woods, they came to a grassy clearing. They could see a rollercoaster and ferris wheel ahead. But something much closer drew their attention. It looked like a bullfrog lying face down. They went over to him. Ricky felt the frog's back with his paw.

"Ees he dead?" Tonto asked.

"He's still breathing," Ricky said and gently rolled him over. "Sick from that water, I betcha."

The frog slowly opened his eyes and took a labored breath. He recoiled when he realized a raccoon was standing over him.

"Oh, Lord, forgive me," the frog said, then hiccupped, "forgive me all the wrongs I have done you."

"Take it easy, buddy," Ricky said. "We ain't gonna hurt ya."

The frog hiccupped, and they carried him under a tree.

"What's your name, buddy?" Ricky asked.

"Boggy," he said between hiccups.

"Relax, Boggy." Ricky said. "Where you from?"

Boggy's long tongue rolled out as he took a deep breath.

"Up north," he said, squelching an urge to hiccup and lick his upperlip, "about 100 miles from here, in the Hotataha Mountains."

"Whatta ya doin down here?"

"I couldn't have any tads back home," said Boggy, his tongue slithering out.

"Dodds?" asked Tonto, who thought Boggy's long tongue reminded him of someone.

"Tadpoles, baby frogs, kids of my own."

"Why jew no can haf doddpoles?" Tonto asked.

"The pollution they call acid rain," Boggy said.

"Gee," Ricky said. "I didn't know pollutans made it so ya couldn't have kids."

"That's what's so bad about it," Boggy said and licked his lip. "It comes from the gases factories put in the air. It gets in the clouds and comes down when it rains. It's especially bad for frogs because we're in the water so much and breathe it through our skin, and fish too, who breathe it through their gills."

"But haven't you heard about the new Underground World?" Ricky asked.

"No," Boggy said. "Not up where I come from."

"Underground, there's lots of clean, pure streams," Ricky said, "and they're all being connected to the Great Underground River, which is where we're going, to join the Capellini Circus which has relocated there."

"Ohh," Boggy said, seeming a bit revived and sitting up. "A circus? Hmm. Sounds inviting."

"Si," Tonto said. "Why jew no comb weeth us? Maybe jew meet with anodder frog who make wit jew a doddpole."

"Sure, why not?" Boggy said.

Still groggy, Boggy climbed up and straddled Ricky's neck. They headed to the circus.

Chapter Nineteen
The Magic of Edgar Allan

Hulking over a red-lettered, blue-bordered white sign which said "Pee Wee Park" was a magnificent rollercoaster. Its racket alternated between screams of riders and the merry-go-round while aromas of cotton candy, popcorn, and hot dogs filtered through. As people hurried into the amusement park, Tonto, Ricky, and Boggy hid under a bush. They were searching for a burrow that might lead to the underground circus. Behind some daisies not far from the admission booth, they noticed a hole.

Though too small for Ricky, Tonto scooted around a little girl to take a closer look. He saw that it led into a carefully fashioned tunnel and he nodded to Ricky.

"Check it out," Ricky called.

Tonto entered the tunnel and followed it down. Soon he came to a fork and a marker with the words "Capellini Circus" in glowing yellow letters. Another marker pointing upward read "Hungry Harry's Hot Dog Haven." Tonto was hungry. Before his trip east he had never eaten a hot dog, but he had found them "deliciosa." He wished he could get some, but he was excited to tell his friends he had found the way.

"Dere was a marker, it point to dee circus," Tonto said excitedly.

"Great," Ricky said, "now all we need is to find a larger entrance."

Ricky and Tonto searched while Boggy waited in the bushes. Luckily, Tonto met a squirrel who directed him to a rotted-out tree stump where there was a larger entrance. From there, the trio found a network of carefully fashioned tunnels that grew increasingly larger with markers that guided them. Then, they came to a sign that said, `Capellini Circus just ahead.' There they found a gate chiseled into a massive hill of stone with a large wolverine outside. He asked their business, then sniffed them for bad blood before letting them pass.

A short tunnel led to a cavern the size of a stadium, and many small gray tents and one that was red, surrounding a gigantic white tent whose big top nearly reached the cavern's ceiling. Animals were going in and out. The trio went inside and saw performers practicing: a shrew eating fire, a mongoose charming cobras, a crocodile swallowing clocks, squirrels on the flying trapeze.

"Good afternoon," they heard a pipsqueaky voice.

They looked around but did not see its owner.

"Down here," the voice repeated.

They shifted their gaze and saw a tiny black mouse with wire-rimmed glasses. He was dressed in a vested suit and derby like Sherlock Holmes.

"Can I help you?" the mouse said formally.

"Yes," Ricky said. "Do you know Regina Ratchett, the head costumer?"

The mouse smiled and relaxed.

"You must be Ricky?"

"How do you know?" Ricky asked.

The mouse extended his tiny paw.

"I'm Edgar Allan, Gina told me you were coming."

"Edgar Allan?" said Ricky. "You?"

"That's right," Edgar Allan said reassuringly. "Now don't worry about a thing. Just come with me."

They followed, and Tonto whispered to Ricky: "Who dis mouse ees?"

"The circus magician and my aunt's husband," Ricky whispered back.

"But your aunt, she not a raccoon?"

"Of course."

"But he so tiny."

Ricky rolled his eyes and shrugged.

They came to an ordinary-looking gray tent. Outside, a grizzly bear stood guard, and before entering, Edgar Allan introduced them to Grizzard. Inside they found Aunt Regina, a matronly raccoon.

"Ricky," she rose on her hind legs and held out her front legs. "What happened? You were supposed to be here last week."

"I'm sorry, Aunt Regina," he said, hugging her. "I had to take a roundabout route because of the coyotes. They're all through the Oppolohow Trail now."

"How's your father?"

"The same."

"It's a pity. He's never been quite right since your mother died in the accident. Well, that's one good thing about living underground, we don't have to worry about humans running us over with their cars."

Aunt Regina prepared them a nice home-cooked meal. She was a friendly, warm animal. Still, Tonto could not imagine how she and the tiny Edgar Allan could be married for the mouse was no bigger than her paw.

Dinner ended with mint tea, and Edgar Allan, who had changed into a purple robe and had put on a wizard-like cap, took them into his study. The trio squeezed in, having to duck their heads. In the center was a tiny oval table upon which sat an octagon-shaped, glass curio.

Framed in gold, it showcased miniatures so small that Tonto could barely distinguish them. Surrounding the table were numerous small bookcases filled with tiny books, and off to the side, a desk with a lamp.

"What sort of magic ya do, Edgar Allan?" Ricky asked. "Pull rabbits out of hats or birds up your sleeve?"

"No, no, nothing like that," Edgar Allan said. "My magic has been passed down through my family for centuries. Remember . . . Alice? She was transported by such magic. As was Gulliver. Both entered that realm where whole universes can reside on the head of a pin."

This puzzled the trio.

"Now, prepare yourself for this," Edgar Allan said.

They froze in astonishment as he transformed and his became voice eerie. He sprinkled them with liquid from a small vial.

"Mice become rats who turn into gnats," he recited. "Bats become bigger than cats; eagles will shrink and the sky will fall;

no creature nor mountain will be too tall. Let them be, relativity."

Simultaneously, all except Edgar Allan shrunk until they were the size of the miniatures and were transported upon the table with the curio.

"Arrima!" cried Tonto, who could not believe such a thing possible and scratched his nose to see if it were real. The table seemed as high as a tall tree and compared to them now, Edgar Allan was a giant.

"You see," said Edgar Allan, "it matters neither how big nor small you are, but how vast is your imagination. Now I will join you."

Edgar Allan sprinkled the potion on himself.

"To universes on heads of pins," he recited, "I am not small, I am not tall. Let me be, relativity."

Instantly, Edgar Allan was the size of the others and transported onto the table with them.

Tonto felt better now. He gazed up at the curio. He could see the miniatures clearly. There were four shelves of them, including a horn of plenty, a unicorn, two golden frogs, a rocking chair, a bouquet of flowers coming from an Aladdin's Lamp, and a rodent dressed like Robin Hood playing a flute, and on top, a female chipmunk dressed in a royal purple robe and holding a violin and balancing on a wire.

"The miniatures hold the secret to my family's magic," Edgar Allan said. "For centuries they have been collected and passed down. They're my most prized possessions."

Edgar Allan laughed as if mentally-ill, and then with a gesture of his finger brought the miniatures to life. While able to move about, it appeared that they could not escape the curio. Tonto's gaze shifted to the chipmunk on the wire, balancing on one foot, her forelegs holding the violin in one paw, and her bow in the other. His heart melted.

"But let us return to normal," he said.

After returning the miniatures to suspended animation, Edgar sprinkled some of the magic potion on himself and them again, then recited, "Rah-Ree-Roo! -- Restore, Revert, Reverse!"

Immediately, they were transported off the table and returned to their normal size.

"So, tell me, boys," Edgar Allan asked, sounding again like his pipsqueaky self, "what kind of work are you looking for here?"

"I'm trying out for apprentice ringmaster," Ricky said.

Boggy and Tonto, however, were unsure of what to say.

"How about you, Boggy? Tonto? Well, would either of you be interested in working with me? I need an assistant."

Boggy shook his head, but Tonto was not so sure. Of course, he was frightened by the powers of Edgar Allan, but he wanted to know more about the chipmunk, and this was his chance.

"Si, si," Tonto said. "Eet soun good to me."

"Then I'll keep you in mind," Edgar Allan said.

At bedtime a small tent was provided, and Aunt Regina made some hot chocolate. Tonto felt like a young dog in his hole on the prairie at Christmas Eve. He had heard so much about the circus: the amazing performers, the bizarre spectacles, the flurry of activity, the travel to exotic places -- but he never expected anything like the magic of Edgar Allan.

Chapter Twenty

Arrima

At the circus the next day, the standing-room only crowd found Tonto, Boggy, and Ricky in the front row munching wildly on popcorn. Out to the center of the Big Top came Maestro Capellini, a white fox with a thin moustache in black tails and top hat. Cheers exploded. Then it quieted.

"Ladies and gentlemen," the Maestro said, "Girls and boys. Welcome to the Capellini Circus."

Everyone was buying popcorn. In fact, the vendors never remembered such a rush.

"Today under the big top," Capellini said, "you will laugh, delight, shout, and leap in amazement at the skills you are about to witness. Now, sit back, open your mind, and let the Capellini Circus take you away!"

The band broke into Julius Fucik's "Entry of the Gladiators."

Three jeeps driven by red foxes circled the arena with bubble machines. Soon the big top was a blizzard of bubbles. Into it came a column of anteaters ridden by lemmings, followed by a column of crocodiles balancing clocks on their snouts, a family of skunks atop a pumpkin-shaped coach pulled by a team of badgers, a smiling shrew with white hair and a white beard, a mongoose alongside a slithering cobra, and an armadillo in a red aerobics suit.

A brief lull in the procession was quickly filled by a chipmunk trapeze artist. She was dressed in a royal purple robe, just like the chipmunk Tonto had seen among Edgar Allan's miniatures. Tonto looked closer. He thought he was seeing things. He could've sworn she looked exactly like her!

Last in the procession was Edgar Allan. Sporting a purple cape and gold conehead cap, he rode atop the neck of Grizzard and made a special point to wave to the boys. After Edgar Allan had come and gone, Maestro Capellini dashed back to center ring.

"Ladies and gentlemen, boys and girls," Capellini said. "Our first attraction is a new act with the Capellini Circus. Direct from the land of Prunes and Dried Apricots, where she was billed as the greatest circus act of our time."

A drum roll started.

"Now under the Big Top, the chameleon on the high wire, whose music enchants everyone and whose amazing balance excels all others -- the amazing Reee-muh!"

The brass blared; the cymbals clashed. Out came the tiny chipmunk. The crowd screamed and everything shook under the tent as she raised her arm above her head.

"Arrima," Tonto mumbled softly.

Yes, it was her, the chipmunk from the curio and she scampered to the rope leading to the high wire. She grasped  the rope and bowed, then was pulled up.

"Ladies and gentlemen!" Capellini announced, and the crowd quieted. "The amazing Rima will perform a feat no one else has ever done or attempted. Not only will she balance herself on one leg, but at the same time, she will play her violin!"

A violin and violin bow were hoisted. Rima rose on her hind legs, took the bow in one paw and the violin in the other. She shuffled onto the high wire and followed with several nimble steps into the center of it. She stopped. The drums quieted. The crowd hushed. Slowly, she raised her right hind leg.

"Ladies and gentlemen!" Capellini broke the silence. "The amazing Rima will now perform the opening movement of Wieniawski's Second Concerto."

She raised her bow and began to play. Her sound was pure, her touch light, her pitch perfect, her paw work nimble, her rhythm danceable, and her balance -- incredible. The way she played, the feeling and love she poured into it made Tonto's heart quiver. At such moments time no longer exists and nothing matters before or after, for this is life as it's meant to be.

"Tonto, Tonto, Tonto," Ricky cried, shaking him, "Snap out of it!"

"Arrima," he uttered.

"Are you okay, Tonto?" Ricky said and laughed.

Tonto felt like a soaring bird. If anyone had told him that love at first sight existed only in fairy tales, he would've told them they were wrong.

During the following acts, Tonto became restless. He got up and went backstage, hoping he might see her. In the wings, he saw stagehands, performers waiting their turn, and clowns. His eyes searched hungrily. Then he spotted the royal purple. He looked up at the face. It was her, staring out, at the show. He moved closer and gazed at her tiny profile and big black eyes. He snapped a mental picture, shrunk up his shoulders, and turned away. Nervous flutterings skipped through him as he turned back and faced her.

"Arrima," he said, feeling like a glob of jelly. "I mean, Me-Mees Uh, Rrima. My name ees . . . Don, Don, Dondoritho. I new here. May be, we . . . be amigos?"

She smiled and extended her paw.

"If thou please, kind sir," she said. "Take thy leave forthwith."

"Ay, okay, Mees, of course," Tonto said and backed away.

"Until the hour of our next meeting, Dondoritho, the Lord be with thee," she said, and waved good-bye.

Tonto slowly retreated. From a safe distance, he watched Grizzard take her away. He was certain now that she was the miniature whom he saw at Edgar Allan's. And the way she went with Grizzard made him worry that the magician night be doing something terrible to her. But what was it about her that drew him to her? The glitter in her eyes, some power she had? Was it a coincidence that his favorite exclamation "Arrima" was a word he had made up as a child?

Tonto returned to where Rima had been standing. On the ground, he spotted a locket.

Inside was a painting of a grand castle and below a tiny inscription: "Amram: Where music is everywhere and all the time."

Going back to his friends in the audience, he began humming his "Mek Beelif" love song.

Chapter Twenty-One
Learning the Magic Words

In the next days the circus traveled by caravan along the Great Underground River to their next destination. Not once did Tonto see Rima. No one had. To console himself, he would open her locket and look at the castle and the inscription. It made him feel her close by.

The day they arrived at their new destination, Aunt Regina made a nice dinner. Tonto wanted so badly to go into Edgar Allan's study but didn't dare ask. He was glad he hadn't because as they dined, Grizzard caught a snooping cat outside and broke its legs. But then the fortuitous break he had hoped for, came. Edgar Allan asked him to be his assistant.

The next day, his first on the job, he arrived early. He was nervous as he greeted Grizzard.

"Edgar Allan is in his study," Grizzard said. "But you may go inside and wait in the kitchen."

He smelled incense and heard a voice coming from the magician's study. It sounded as if Edgar Allan were talking to someone. The conversation didn't last long, however, and Edgar Allan came out to welcome him. He poured them a cup of mint tea, and ushered Tonto into his study. After some sips of tea, he recited the magic words, his voice transforming into the deeper, eerie tone Tonto had heard before.

"Mice become rats who turn into gnats. Bats become bigger than cats; eagles will shrink and the sky will fall; no creature nor mountain will be too tall. Let Tonto be, relativity."

Tonto became Edgar Allan's size. He looked at the miniatures and could see that there was no doubt now that the miniature aloft over the curio was indeed Rima. He pulled a chair alongside Edgar Allan.

"As my assistant, Tonto, you will learn to do magic. This is required to perform your duties. However, you must pledge never to use this magic without my permission. Otherwise, you could cause harm. Is that clear?"

Tonto nodded.

"Now, the most important part of your job is to provide for the safety and care of my miniatures."

Tonto's ears perked up and he glanced up at Rima, wondering if she remembered him or could tell that he was there, or thinking perhaps that she might be completely frozen in time and as if asleep.

"You must swear never to reveal anything about your work with them," Edgar Allan said sternly. "This is very important, because from time to time, I bring the miniatures to life to perform for the circus. Perhaps you noticed that the tightrope walker, Rima, is identical to the miniature up there in my collection?"

Edgar Allan laughed like the Frankenstein monster.

"Well, that is no accident. They are one and the same."

Edgar Allan raised his paw, and Tonto watched in amazement as Rima floated gently down to the table. However, she remained frozen in her pose.

"You must assist the miniatures after they have been revitalized. You will assist them during their performances and afterwards escort them back to my study. Then you will return them to their former state. Let me demonstrate."

Edgar Allan sprinkled potion on Rima.

"Oh, yes, before I forget. The cup of mint tea I drank is always required before any magic can be performed. Its power is a little-known secret and without imbibing it into your system, you will not be able to perform the magic. Never forget that."

Tonto nodded, and Edgar Allan placed his paw over Rima, and recited a different set of magic words: "Let the life that lies in wait, resume its breath to abate. Make the heart of this being, Rima, beat strong and give her vitality. La-Loh-Lee . . . Life-for-thee!"

Edgar Allan poured a dash of powder in his paw and blew it on Rima. Instantly, she came to life.

"To universes on heads of pins, Rima is not small, we are not tall. Let Rima be, relativity."

Edgar Allan raised his front right leg, following through as if throwing a ball at Rima, and she assumed the relative size of Tonto and Edgar Allan.

"How's my little dear Rima?" Edgar Allan said.

She smirked.

"I want you to meet someone. This is Tonto, my new assistant."

Rima smiled broadly and held out her paw.

" 'Tis a pleasure to meet thee, Tonto," Rima said, her eyes lingering with his in recognition.

Tonto returned her smile and grasped her paw gently.

"He will be helping you with your act," Edgar Allan said, "and escorting you to and from the Big Top. Is that clear?"

Rima nodded.

"That is all," Edgar Allan said.

Without so much as a good-bye, Edgar Allan reduced Rima and returned her to a state of suspended animation above the curio. Then, after a few more words about his duties, Edgar Allan told Tonto to return at 5 o'clock to prepare for the night's performance.

When Tonto returned to Edgar Allan's study, Rima already had been made normal size and was waiting for him with Edgar Allan.

"Now, Tonto," Edgar Allan said, handing him instructions with the magic words. "You will bring Rima here before the circus ends and I will meet you to show you how to return her to the curio. Okay? I will see you both later."

The magician excused himself to prepare for his act, leaving Tonto and Rima alone. Tonto became nervous. On impulse, he blurted out his feelings.

"I theenk I loaf jew, Mees Rrima," he said.

Rima turned away.

"Such declarations, dear dog, shouldst not come from thy lips," she said.

"I sorry. But is wrong to say dis?"

She took a deep breath.

" 'Tis not wise to speak here. Let us go forth," she said.

Outside, away from the tent and Grizzard, Rima spoke more openly.

"We must take care what be said betwixt us, Tonto. The sorcerer's powers are great. 'Twould not surprise me if he were able to hear our every word."

"I no care. I will make jew free no madder what hees powers."

"Nay, Tonto. 'Tis not so easy. To unchain my fetters, thou must gain the knowledge of his magic. Such, could be long in coming."

"Why are jew hees pree-so-ner?"

"Whilst I grieved over my betrothed, whose death messengers had brought word from his expedition, of a sudden I found mineself in the state of a statue, and on the ledge below, and likewise, mine betrothed."

"Eees true you leaved een a castle in a place called Amram?" Tonto asked.

"How dost thou know?"

"I fine your locket on dee groun dat day I see jew," he said, and took it out.

"So, thou dost understand that I come hither from a place not of this time?"

"I not was chure. But I know now. And of chore be- . . ."

"Betrothed, Tonto," Rima finished his sentence. "My betrothed, my Cisco stands frozen now in the curio."

Rima pointed to a ledge in the curio and a miniature of a man with a bow and arrow. He was dressed like Robin Hood, with a flute sticking up from the middle of the pouch of arrows that was slung over his shoulder.

"It no madder," he said. "I will help jew both."

" 'Twill not be a thing of ease, Tonto. If thou dost try, and Edgar Allan catches wind, thou shalt become likewise his prisoner."

After the circus, in the presence of Edgar Allan, Tonto returned Rima to her place with the other miniatures. All the while, his mind raced with thoughts of freeing Rima. He wondered if Edgar Allan could tell. That night he tossed and turned in bed. He had nightmares that he had become a miniature himself.

Chapter Twenty-Two
Only Make Believe

Though Tonto now had been entrusted with the power to animate and re-size Rima, he did not have the power to free her. But Rima had told him about a magic book in the study that the magician often consulted. Perhaps, it would reveal some of Edgar Allan's powers. And though he realized the danger, he could not bear to see Rima frozen in that curio. Finally, he told Ricky and Boggy about the true nature of Edgar Allan.

"I learn very bad teeng a-bout Edgar Allan," he said.

"I'm not surprised," Ricky said.

"Yeah," Boggy added, "I never trusted him."

"So, what d'ya find out?" Ricky asked.

"Edgar Allan has animal in slavery," Tonto said.

"Slavery? Where?" Ricky said.

"Hees box of leedle ting. Do jew not realize dat leedle Rrima dee tightrope walker is one and dee same with hees mee-nee-ture acrobat? I haf seen her come back to life and I talk with her. Chee tell me Edgar Allan put a spell on her and all dee odder een dee box."

"Come to think of it, I thought I recognized her," Ricky said.

"That's right," Boggy said, "now that you mention it. She's the one above the curio."

Tonto thought for a moment. He wanted so much to help Rima, but he knew he would need help.

"I wonder eef mebbee jew will help me make her free?" Tonto asked.

"I'd have to mull that one over," Ricky said. "Not that I don't believe you, but this Edgar Allan feller's damn sight powerful. I wouldn't want to get him mad at me, or you. Let me talk to my aunt."

"Be careful what you say to her, Ricky," Boggy said. "Edgar Allan could put a spell on all of us, and her too."

Ricky talked to Regina. However, she was reluctant to talk about the magician. This convinced Ricky that something was wrong, and he and Boggy agreed to help Tonto. They devised a plan in which they would ask Edgar Allan to take them and Regina to Pee Wee Park, while Tonto would stay behind, pretending to be sick.

The next day Ricky, Boggy, Edgar Allan, and Regina went aboveground to Pee Wee Park. Now that they were gone, all Tonto had to do was get rid of Grizzard, whom he knew would be guarding Edgar Allan's tent. He decided to brew a cup of tea and add knockout drops, which he got from the crocodile trainer. He went to Edgar Allan's tent.

"My amigo, Grizzard," Tonto slapped paws. "How jew like a cop of meent tea, today, ay?"

Grizzard, who enjoyed a good cup of tea, smiled, and without hesitation swigged it down. He made an expression of satisfaction, then suddenly slumped and rolled over.

In Edgar Allan's study, Tonto gazed at the curio with the tiny Rima atop it. He located Edgar Allan's magic incense and put some in the burner. He scooped up more and showered Rima with it, then recited the magic words:

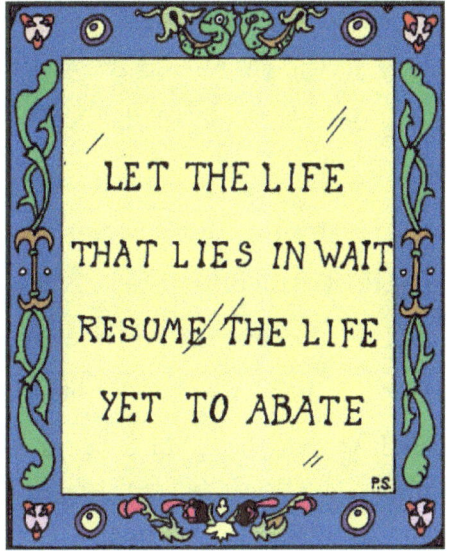

"Let dee life dat lie in wait, resume eets breath yet to a-bate. Mek dee heart of dis being, Rrima, beat strong and gif her vitality. Lah-Loh-Lee-Life-for-thee."

Again, Tonto sprinkled incense on Rima and she came alive, though still in miniature.

"My dear Tonto," she said, "thou hast become a magician!"

"I know I could make dee magic, mees. And I haf aynother surprise for jew. Edgar Allan, he ees away for all dee day, so now we try for jew eh-scape.

"Thy pluck is worthy, Tonto. But dost thou understand full well the danger?"

"Would jew rather we no try?"

She didn't answer, and Tonto recited the magic words.

"Mice becomb rats who turn eento gnat. Bats become beeger dan cat; eagle will shrink and dee sky weel fall; no creature nee mounteen will be too tall. Let Rrima be, rela-tee-vee-tee."

Tonto waved his arms, and Rima became his size.

"The deed be done, Tonto," she said. "Now, free Cisco."

Tonto peered into the curio at Cisco. He sprinkled potion on him. Then recited the words: Let dee life dat lie in wait, resume eets breath yet to a-bate. Mek dee the heart of dis being, Ceesco, beat strong and gif heem vitality. La-Loh-Lee-Life-for-thee."

Cisco stirred, and Tonto continued with the words.

"To jew-knee-verses on head of peen. Ceesco is no small. Ceesco is no tall. Let Cee-sco be, rela-tee-vee-tee."

In a swoosh, Cisco hopped out of the curio and became normal size. He raced up to Rima, and reached out and tried to kiss her paw, but she pulled away.

"Forgive me, my fair Rima," he said, bowing his head at her feet. "Thou sweet love, more luscious than the grapes upon heaven's gates. Thou wondrous creature, whose music is more lovely than any  lullaby. Thou art mine only true love. Without thee and thine music, dearest Rima, I cannot go on."

"Tush, Cisco," Rima broke in. "Thou thinkest fine words can bring my favors? Nay, Cisco. Thou wilt need more."

"But my Lady."

"If at some later time, I so deem, I shall consider it. First, we must needs make our return to Amram."

Cisco continued to plead.

"I pray thee, dearest Rima, be so kind as to hear my tale before we depart."

"After our return," Rima said. "Rather, the sorcerer's book must be consulted!"

As she had seen Edgar Allan do so many times, Rima slipped the heavy book out of the bookcase which hid the space where he kept his magic book. Then she recited the words she had memorized: "Magic book, reveal thine hiding place!"

In the formerly vacant spot, a safety deposit box materialized. She opened it and found the magic book. She put it on the desk and turned to the index.

"Let us search the entry for Time," she said. "Ha! The alteration of time and place, page 777."

She flipped through the pages as Cisco and Tonto edged closer, looking over her shoulder.

"How to leave one place and go to another," she read aloud." `How to leave one time and go to another; how to leave both time and place and go to another time and place in the snap of a finger.' Ay, that be it!"

She continued to read.

"To get to a particular time and place, one must capture its essence in heartfelt thoughts, words, and deeds. One must also possess a material link, that is, a relic that existed in that time and place like a piece of clothing or wood. The minutest portion is sufficient. With the relic in one's possession, one must wait for a celestial manifestation. Then, at the precise moment, one must recite the following words: Let all that is good, be whole, once again . . ."

Cisco interrupted: "The good Lord be with us. Our very clothes can take us home. Let us sally forth!"

"Let us not be so hasty," Rima says. "For it counsels that with such relics, one can recall persons wherever or whenever they may be. We should be sure that he not hath kept such relics of our persons."

"Let us begin our search," Cisco said.

"Or better," Rima said, "let us consult the book."

Again Rima turned to the index and found the heading, `Hiding Estimables.' She turned to the pages listed for the appropriate commands. After she recited them, they found Edgar Allan had hidden relics of all those enslaved. This aroused Rima's sympathies, and in one quick recitation, she freed the others in the curio. They gathered around, and one of the frogs was their spokesperson.

"Thank you," said the bull frog, and the others murmured their approval.

"Thy gratitude is well taken," Rima said.

A muffled voice came from inside the Aladdin's lamp, which was one of the miniatures in the curio.

"The lamp needs some rubbing, I think," the bull frog said, and Rima and the bull frog went to the lamp and began rubbing. In a puff of smoke, out came the genie wearing a turban with a large sapphire pinned in front.

"Thank you! Thank you! Thank you!" the genie bellowed repeatedly.

"You're quite welcome," Rima and the bull frog said.

"I'm glad we're all now free," the genie said. "I must hurry back to my time and place, where rajahs have harems and men play flutes in marketplaces, and the women wear veils and are adorned by the most precious jewels in all the world. Any of you who wish to join me, are quite welcome."

Only the unicorn decided to join the genie; the others stayed with Rima, Cisco, and Tonto. But Tonto now had mixed feelings. His heart felt numb since Cisco had come alive. If he stayed, however, Edgar Allan would punish him severely. Perhaps this was part of his necessary journey.

Chapter Twenty-Three
A Most Ethereal Firmament

In the horizon above the subterranean world, along a woodland pond under marshmallow clouds, Rima tuned up her violin and Cisco, his flute. At the first sign of the celestial manifestation, they would play and Tonto would recite while the others watched and waited.

"My Rima," Cisco said, "now while we wait for the manifestation, 'tis an advantageous time to recite my tale."

"Ay," Rima said, "thy tale should prove worthy. Tell it to me."

"I met a soothsayer," Cisco said. "He spoke of a place where death is banished, and pledged to send us there together. He had no foreknowledge of the sorcery of Edgar Allan."

"Ha," Rima said, "And that is why I came to be here?"

" 'Tis true," Cisco said. " 'Twas I who entrusted thine locket in his possession. And for such, I ask thee forbearance."

Rima did not answer. Instead, she turned to Tonto and the others.

"Thou must wonder about our homeland?" she said.

"Si," Tonto said.

"Yes, what is it like?" asked one of the bull frogs.

"Harmonious," Rima said. "In our world, humans and animals make music together."

"Ow can dat be?" Tonto asked.

"It harketh back to a time forgotten, when animals and humans possessed the same language," Rima said. " 'Tis why our land knoweth harmony. And 'tis nothing more, we need petition."

"My dear Rima, I must lodge my disagreement," Cisco said. "Thine absence has clouded thine memory. Thine eyes glossed over. Amram possessed a goodly share of unhappiness."

"In thine eyes, perhaps, Cisco," she said. "But thou art one who looks for such things."

"Be that as it may," Cisco said. "To me 'tis clear as the brightest star. That without fail in every place, cometh a time for the end of that time."

"Luke!" Tonto cried. "A black curteen, she's covereeng dee sun!"

Rima and Cisco took up their instruments and Tonto opened the book to the precise page.

"Let us commence the ceremony," Rima said.

Rima and Cisco played a duo for violin and flute while Tonto read: "Let all dat ees good, be whole, once again. Let dee loafs dat we know dat leave forever, return. Let dee moments of time reassemble. Let dee eternal recurrence manifest."

After Tonto finished, Cisco took a smaller flute-like instrument from inside his jacket and inserted it in the left side of his mouth. He took another like a kazoo and inserted it in the right side of his mouth. Then he picked up his flute and played all three instruments at once.

The music made Tonto buoyant. He started to tap his hind paws. Suddenly, Rima dropped her violin, which continued playing by itself. She grabbed Tonto's forepaws and led him in a dance, like a waltz, but faster, and they were joined by the other former miniatures. Soon Tonto was dancing as if he had been dancing all his life. Like dreidels, they all swirled around, then spun off and tumbled to the ground. Bursting into laughter, they looked up at Cisco who had stopped playing.

"Why have we not left this place!" Cisco shouted. "We did as instructed yet have moved not a stone's throw!"

A massive black cloud rolled over the horizon and fog moved in. When they could barely see a few feet in front of them, a gust of wind whistled through. It dispersed the fog, and the sun shown on a new landscape.

"The Lord be with us!" Cisco shouted.

" 'Tis a miracle indeed!" Rima added. "Look! A procession for the dead coming up the hill."

"Ay, we are in Amram," Cisco said.

The other miniatures cheered as they watched the procession led by a girl pulling a wagon with a harp. Following her were both animals and humans, all carrying musical instruments and candles. The girl, dressed in a frilly white gown with a lace collar, stopped. A huge smile formed on her face.

"My Lady! My Lord!" she called and bounded towards them.

"Lacy!" Rima said, then hugged her friend.

"Mine eyes believe not what they see!" said Lacy, whose chubby cheeks brightened with color. "Our purpose in coming to the holy hill was to make music in thine memory. And now, look at thee! Where? Where hast thou been?"

"We were held captive," Rima said, "but later I will tell the tale. Rather, why not we make the music thou intended?"

"What of your friend? What might be his instrument?"

"Let me introduce Tonto," Rima said. "Tonto, I present Lacy."

Lacy curtsied and Tonto smiled.

"Without the assistance of Tonto, we would not be here," Cisco interjected. "And for that I shall forever remain in his debt."

"And thou hast an instrument?" asked Lacy.

"Eenstrument? Me? Arrima, I no play eenstrument."

"Be not alarmed, Tonto," Rima said. "In Amram everyone can play an instrument, and we have just the one for you, Tonto."

She looked at Lacy.

"Do we not, Lacy?"

Lacy nodded and smiled as the other orchestra members took their places. There were house cats with violins, giant bugs with violas, cows and elephants with horns, frogs with bassoons, and a flock of birds with flutes and oboes. From behind Tonto, came a tap on his shoulder. He turned and saw a giant, green, purple spotted caterpillar alongside Rima.

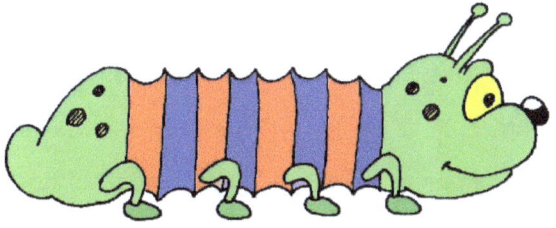

"Thine instrument, kind sir," Rima said. "Tonto, permit me to introduce thee to my dear friend, Alfred."

"My pleasure," Alfred said.

"Alfred is a Russian caterpillar," Rima said.

"I come from Moldavia, Mees Rima," Alfred said, "but plees, go ahead."

"Alfred is a born musician," Rima explained, "one who feeleth music in every part of his body, from the tip of his antenna to the end of his abdomena. Truly, a living musical instrument."

"Absolutely," Alfred said.

"So, Meester Alfred weel jew chowe me ow to play dee eenstrument?" Tonto asked.   "Absolutely,"   Alfred repeated.

"But I no see eenstrument."

Rima shook her head.

"Clean out thine ears, Tonto," she said, " 'Tis Alfred who is thine instrument."

"Alfred?"

"Ay," Rima said. "And to play him is a task of joy and ease. Just squeeze him and the music cometh forth.   Let me demonstrate."

Rima picked up Alfred, holding one end in one paw and the other in another, the way one would hold an accordion.

"Now, fix thine eyes as I squeeze," she said and demonstrated, causing a blend of sound to come out of him. "And now, pull on him."

Another phrase of sounds ushered forth.

"Is it not simple?" Rima said. "The key is to follow the lead of his bodily rhythms, then let him take over, correct Alfred?"

"Absolutely," Alfred said. "Just squeeze vibrations you feel, Tonto. It eez quite yeezy if you approach like teamwork, of feeling and leestening vid your soul."

Rima gave Alfred to Tonto. A baton was handed to her, and she stepped up on a stool behind a podium. She tapped the baton against the podium to get everyone's attention. They quieted and she addressed them.

"Animals, friends, and Amrammers, how wonderful to see you. Thou cannot imagine the wonderful music I learned whilst in captivity, and now we will have all the time we need to learn it. First, Cisco and I wish to demonstrate our gratefulness to the prairie dog, Tontoritho He-mayonnaise with the gift of music. Never forget, Tonto, thou will ever be close to mine heart."

Tonto blushed. He smiled at Rima as the orchestra members applauded.

"In honor of his valiant efforts," she said, "let us accompany him as he playeth Alfred. Now, please take notice of the music in front of thee. 'Tis one of the new pieces I learned. Use Alfred's lead to follow. Then, let the rhythm take thee away!"

Tonto stiffened.

"I no chure I can do eet, Meester Alfred," he whispered.

"Do not vurry, Tonto," Alfred said, "just follow me and you vill not have trrouble."

Rima raised her baton and nodded to Tonto and Alfred.

"Okay, Tonto," Alfred whispered, following with a convulsion.

Out came four notes, followed by a variation of the first four, and then another variation. Tonto noticed that rather than squeeze Alfred he needed only to hold on and let him do the rest. The other musicians joined in and Tonto found it rather easy to follow Alfred's gyrations, and yet it was as if he were the one playing and the one with the rhythm. Soon he felt as if sailing through space without a care. It was that special pleasure all music lovers come to realize, after which they experience it, their lives are never the same again. Oh, if you could only hear it, if only everyone could hear it. You would never *ask for anything more?*

When the music ended, there was applause from the other musicians. Tonto felt chills as he put down Alfred, who responded with "Bravos."

"Brravo, Tonto, brravo."

"Take a bow, Tonto," Rima shouted through the uproar. "No one deserves it more."

Tonto took his bows. He felt elation, but also a nagging at the back of his mind. Someone telling him that making heavenly music was what "it" was all about. As the applause continued, everything began to blur for Tonto. He felt the need to lie down. He rolled over on his side and closed his eyes.

"You traitor! You ungrateful little dog!"

Tonto thought he was dreaming. He opened his eyes. Hovering over him was the huge head of Edgar Allan, who was so much bigger than he had ever seen him while Tonto was so much smaller than he normally was. Tonto was lying in front of the empty curio. On the table, he noticed a pair of his plaid underpants. Edgar Allan must've used them to bring him back.

"You may have saved your friends, you filthy dog, but not yourself. Now I'm going to turn you into a jar of mayonnaise and mix you in a tuna fish salad!"

Edgar Allan growled, but Tonto thought of the command to return himself to normal size and noticed the magician's mug of tea on the desk. In one motion, he jumped into it, swallowing some as he went under. As his head bobbed back, he recited the magic words: "To jew-knee-verses on head of peen, I no small, I no tall. Let me be, rela-tee-vee-tee."

Tonto was launched out of the cup and onto the floor full-size. Bigger than Edgar Allan now, he took the shocked magician in his mouth and tossed him against a bookcase. Making sure to take his underpants, he dashed out of the study. Tonto scurried away until he came to an intersection of tunnels. Rather than taking the one which led back to the amusement park, he took a different road. He had no idea where it led, but anywhere was fine so long as it was away from Edgar Allan. He started to think about Rima and hummed his "mek beelif" love song.

The tunnel snaked up and down, right and left, and there were many branches. Tonto picked his route at random. At some points it was pitch dark, in other sections very bright. He had gone a great distance before he stopped to rest. His thoughts continued to dwell on Rima. If only he could retrieve the magic book and return to Amram. But he did have her locket. Perhaps, someday, it would help him get back to Amram. That is, if somehow he could find another magic book.

When he resumed his journey, he came to a 45-degree incline. He crawled up and up, and at times had to burrow through the dirt. Finally, he saw a pinprick of distant light. It got bigger as he headed towards it. He moved faster. The light opened out of the side of a rolling, hilly landscape. Ahead, was a large pasture filled with grazing cows, a barn, a farmhouse, and couple of other buildings. Drawing closer, he smelled something rotten. Then came a hideous scream. Dogs started barking. He scurried under a bush.

Shaking uncontrollably, Tonto shot out from the cover of the bush away from the farm, only to find two Dobermans racing towards him from that direction. He tried to recite one of the magic commands, but it was useless without the mint tea. Fleeing back towards the farm, he slipped under the foundation of a building just before the dogs got there. The smell was even more disgusting now, but he was trapped. His heart palpitated as the barking dogs were dispersed by a farmer.

Catching his breath, he peeked inside the building. The walls were painted white and the floor covered with sawdust. A half-dozen cows were lined up inside a narrow stall that led to an enclosed area.

The cows seemed restless; their ears wiggled and their heads bobbed. From the enclosed area came another shriek. The cows tried to turn, but the stalls kept them in place. Tonto scurried along the edge of the foundation towards the area cut off from his sight. He peeked in. It was too ghastly to describe as well as incredible: the creatures, who were slaughtering the cows, had the bodies of humans and the heads of hyenas! Tonto felt sick to his stomach and feared for his life like never before.

He had to get away. He crept back to the other side and waited for nightfall. His thoughts returned to Rima, and he took out her locket and pressed it to his heart. As the sun set, the slaughter of the cows stopped, and the workmen departed. He closed his eyes and fell asleep.

When he awoke, it was pitch black and crickets and cicadas were clacking. Except for the occasional whimper of a dog, there was no sound and everything was stillness. What better time to get away. Taking a deep breath, Tonto snuck his head out. He looked and listened. Not a sound. He stepped, one paw at a time, then broke into a sprint. His heart sped like never before, and then he dropped something. Rima's locket. He stopped. It was too dark to see where. A dog barked, then another, then came a cacophony of barks.

Tonto took off without the locket. He couldn't outrun them now. He stopped and looked for a hole in which to escape. Frantic, he started to burrow one. But before he made headway, a huge Doberman lunged at him and took him in his jaws. The dog did not bite down but merely held him. Tonto's whole body rattled as the dog took him back. Awaiting was the human-like hyena master with a pitchfork, his tongue hanging over his knife-like teeth.

"Hey-hey-hey-hey!" the hyena howled as the Doberman presented Tonto to him.

"Good boy, George," he said to the Doberman. "He will add flavor to our hot dogs. Now put him down."

The dog dropped him, and Tonto watched the farmer raise his pitchfork.

"No!" Tonto cried. "Pliss, Senor!"

The hyena showed no mercy and the hyena thrust the pitchfork into Tonto's side. Again and again, he jabbed. With each blow, the pain lessened. In a short time, Tonto's life had seeped away.

Dying was like falling asleep. But he wasn't asleep. He was in pieces in a box. It was unloaded and carried into a room. The box was opened, and his pieces were dumped into a huge funnel, which drew him into a rotary of saws and blades. Soon he was nothing but minced meat, oozing out of a sausage shaped tube into a deep cart.

When the cart was filled, he was transported to a huge vat into which various liquids and spices were also dumped. Like one of those whips in an amusement park, he was churned around until blended into a thick paste. Then through a complex of machinery with dips and turns and conveyors this paste of life was taken where it was apportioned and stuffed into skins. After being wrapped in a clear plastic package and labeled, it was put on an assembly line. His destination was a loading point where he was placed into a bigger box, which was piled into a refrigerator truck.

Chapter Twenty-Four

A Dandy Dog

"Heyyy, red hots! Red hots here. Heyyy, get your red hots! Red hots here!" a voice shouted into Tonto's hazy awareness.

But he wasn't Tonto anymore. Whatever he was and wherever he was, it was so dark he couldn't see a thing. And ohh, was it hot, like being in a steam bath -- a steam bath that smelled of hot dogs.

Suddenly, light shone in as the cover above lifted. Now he could tell that he was a hot dog in a pile of other dogs, all of them unwrapped and being cooked by the steam. Over a public address system, he could hear: "The next batter for the Dandies is number 12, the shortstop, Mel McGonigle."

There were whistles and hoots. Then a pair of metal tongs grabbed hold of him and placed him on a roll. The vendor slobbered mustard all over him.

"Enjoy your Dandy Dog," the vendor said, passing him to a little boy. In one motion, the boy put him up to his mouth and chomped off a bite. It was almost like the time the cricket Charcccazee was eaten by that bird. Except before the boy had even finished the hot dog, the dog felt as if he could see, feel, and jump around just like a boy. But not just any boy. He was Charles again!

He pinched himself, then reached atop his head. He had on his Dandy ball cap. Yes, he really was Charles! All alone at Dandy Stadium in the grandstands where he had sat the last time with his Uncle Vince, just behind the box seats and the Dandy dugout. But even more unbelievable was that squatting on one knee in the on-deck circle was number seven, Nicky Noodle!

The scoreboard showed the bottom of the ninth with the score tied 0-0. The Dandies were up with one out and the bases empty. They were playing the Indians, and Charles recognized the pitcher on the mound, strikeout artist, Wayne HyTouch. McGonigle took a practice swing as Hytouch got the sign.

As HyTouch brought his hands together at his chest, the crowd's chatter died. McGonigle dug his back foot in, and behind Charles a man put his fingers up to his mouth and let out a shrill whistle. Then HyTouch lifted his right leg, wound up, and rifled a fast ball. McGonigle swung and sent a line shot that caromed off HyTouch's head! HyTouch was on the ground! The third baseman dove for the ball as it ricocheted but missed, and McGonigle was safe.

HyTouch was motionless, and players and coaches crowded around him. During this, Charles ran down to the box seats to get a closer look at Noodle. So riveted by what had happened, no one noticed Charles and he stopped just behind the short fence that separated the seats from the field.

While Hytouch was carried off on a stretcher, Charles stared at Noodle swinging four bats. Then Noodle put down the bats and headed back towards the dugout. Charles froze. His whole body tingled. He watched Noodle pass so close that Charles could've touched him. Noodle looked up and his eyes met Charles. And Noodle smiled! Charles couldn't believe it.

Nicky Noodle smiled at him! Charles spun around, then felt someone grab him from behind.

"Ya gotta ticket for this section, boy?" said a man in a uniform man with a wrinkled brown face.

Charles pouted.

"C'mon, let me see your ticket?"

"I think I lost it," Charles said.

"Snuck in, huh?" the man said and puckered his lips. "Well, you just gonna have to git back aways."

The man led Charles by the arm farther back in the box section where there were some vacant seats.

"Okay, now you find yourself a seat up here."

Charles stood there in surprise.

"Did you hear what I said? Go sit down."

Charles funneled into a vacant seat and sat there, his heart thumping. Wow! He had seen Noodle in person up close and Nicky had actually smiled at him! By this time, the famous relief pitcher, Helmut Hillmine, was on the mound warming up. Charles leaned forward on the back of the seat in front of him. He began wondering how he had gotten here and why Nicky Noodle had smiled at him. Then he realized that if this really were Dandy Stadium, he could ask someone to call his Uncle Vince's phone number. He could do this after the game.

Finally, Noodle was at bat. A switch hitter, he was batting right-handed against the left-handed Hillmine. The crowd quieted. Noodle reached out with his bat and took a half swing, and another. Then he went into his classic stance with the bat pointing straight up, gripping at the very end, his fingers squeezing the handle. Hillmine kicked up his right leg and followed through to release a fluttering knuckleball. Noodle stepped into it, dipping his right shoulder. His swing was one blur and miss. The crowd roared.

The catcher threw the ball back. Noodle stepped out of the batter's box. Charles wondered about his parents and if he had been gone that long. Were the police looking for him? Was he going to get in trouble for missing school?

Noodle stepped back in the batter's box and took half swings, and Hillmine nod his head at the sign from the catcher. Hillmine kicked up his leg and let another one float up. Noodle waited, and at the last moment stuck out his bat and bunted. The infield had been way back, and McGonigle had been running on the pitch. The ball rolled up the first base line and Noodle streaked past it. Hillmine raced off the mound, and in motion reached down and flipped the ball to first base. But it went over the first baseman's head down the foul line. Already, McGonigle had rounded second base and the third base coach was waving him on. The right fielder retrieved the ball and fired it home. But it was wide of home plate, and though McGonigle slid, it wasn't necessary. The game was over. The Dandies had won!

After the cheering, the still buzzing crowd shuffled out. Charles's elation was brief. He had to call his Uncle Vince. Down the ramp with the crowd, he saw a man standing in the hallway, dressed in a suit who looked like he might be someone important.

"Hello, sir. I'm trying to contact my uncle. Can you look up his number on your cell phone?"

"What's his name?" the man asked.

"Vincent Cacciatore?"

"Can you spell that?"

"It's C-A-C-C-I-A-T-O-R-E?"

As the man searched his cell phone, Charles wondered what he'd do if he couldn't get his uncle's number, and finally the man said he was unable to find the number.

Charles trudged out of Dandy Stadium into a world of people ignoring one other. He walked along a city block and sat down on steps leading to an apartment building next to a delicatessen. What was he going to do? He didn't know anyone. And this was such a big city.

Charles put his head in his hands. He was sobbing when a tiny old lady noticed. She was shuffling along, bent over by shopping bags in each hand, wearing a long coat and a kerchief around her head. She gazed at Charles, then moved closer and dropped her bags.

"What's the matter, little boy?" she asked.

Charles looked up and whimpered.

"I'm lost. And, and I don't think I'll find my way home, ever!"

He looked down and she patted the back of his head.

"There, there, don't worry. Everything'll be all right."

Charles sniffled.

"What's your name?" she asked.

"Charles," he said.

"Charles?"

"Charles Paganono."

"And where do you live, Charles?"

"In, in Haneckhadee, I think. But I'm not sure anymore. I'm not sure how I even got here."

The old lady shook her head.

"Well," she said, "let me get a policeman for you, and maybe he'll be able to help you." Just then, a bus pulled up, making a loud sneeze. The door opened.

"Just a minute, Ralph," she said to the bus driver, then turned to Charles.

"Now listen, Charles, why don't you come home with me, and I'll see what I can do. I have two grandsons and a granddaughter who live with me. They'd love to meet you. And my brother's best friend is a policeman. I'm sure he'll be able to help."

Charles didn't want to be left alone, so he went with the lady.

Chapter Twenty-Five

Amen

The old lady lived in a two-family house along a row of similar houses with front porches and crewcut lawns. Hanging off her porch was a little wooden sign written in black cursive, The Lasagnas. The lady opened the front door for Charles and followed him inside.

Everything looked as if cloaked in a transparent veil. Hanging on the wall to the left above a mantel was a golden crucifix. It glowed in the blurred light. On the right was an archway that opened to another room.

Sitting on the couch in front of the TV were two boys and a tiny tot of a girl. Their heads spun around and their black eyes, like little bowling balls, glued onto Charles. To him their images looked more like a motion picture than the real thing.

"This is Charles," Grandma Lasagna said to the children. "He lost his way home, so I thought we might be able to help him."

"Sure, Gram," said the bigger boy, who walked over, followed by the others.

"Charles," Grandma said, "these are my grandkids, Joe, Ray, and Mimi."

Mimi laughed. Her big eyes popped out at Charles.

"We're gonna sing in church tomorrow," she said.

Her brothers looked at her and shook their heads. Grandma smiled.

"Charles lost the way home to his mommy and daddy, Mimi," Grandma said. "Where's Uncle Teach?"

"Upstairs," Joe said.

They went into the adjacent dining room. Things started to clear a bit for Charles. Grandma laid her shopping bags on the long table.

"Look what I got, fa-sol-las!"

She pulled out a package of chocolate cookies wrapped in cellophane. Her grandsons looked ready to pounce on them, so she put them back in the bag.

"That's for dessert tonight. Go get Uncle Teach. He's gotta call Tee-dough at the police station for Charles."

The boys left. Mimi leaned against a chair, sucking her thumb, smiling shyly at Charles.

"Now Charles," Grandma said, "soon as Uncle Teach comes down, I'll have him call the police station."

Feet stampeded down the stairs. Uncle Teach Lasagna, a short, bald man wider than he was tall, strutted into the dining room. Behind him were his nephews.

"This is Charles, Teach," said Grandma.

Uncle Teach, who had a chubby, boyish face, smiled at Charles. Grandma took him aside and whispered something, then Uncle Teach spoke to Charles.

"Don't worry, Charles," Teach said in a high-pitched voice. "My friend Tee-dough will help you."

After Uncle Teach called his friend, he said the police were going to run a computer search for persons with the last name of Paganono. Then he suggested that Joe, Ray and Mimi sing for Charles.

"Uncle Teach is a choir director," Grandma said.

"Yeah," Joe said. "And we're gonna sing with the grown-ups in church tomorrow. What's it called, Uncle Teach, the song we're gonna sing?"

"*Verdi's Requiem*," Uncle Teach said.

"Yeah, Charles," Ray said, "we're gonna sing it in church tomorrow."

"But what do you want to sing for Charles now?" Uncle Teach asked.

"Let's sing *Amen*," Joe said.

They agreed and went into the living room, gathering alongside Uncle Teach, who sat down in front of a small organ with two keyboards and lots of buttons. He took his silver pitch pipe out of his shirt pocket and blew a tone on it.

"Dough . . ." they intoned.

"Now, Mimi, before we begin, let's hear your part, "In sempiterna saecula."

Mimi sang in her child-like voice.

You know what that means, Charles?" Uncle Teach asked.

Charles shook his head.

" 'Until the end of all time, forever and forever.' They're very important words, Charles Never forget them."

Uncle Teach turned back to the Lasagna kids.

Okay," he said, and played the opening notes on the organ, then motioned for them to begin.

"Ahh-men!" the children sang. Charles noticed how clear their voices sounded. At the same time, an aura like a halo began to glow around them. He looked around the room and spied two statues of saints on the mantel just below the golden crucifix, and one of the Blessed Virgin on the end table alongside the sofa. Like the Lasagna kids they seemed to give off an aura, and then as if by magic appeared to come alive, like saints used to do long ago. when they made visitations to people. They all seemed to be smiling, like the holy picture on the adjacent wall of Christ pointing to his sacred heart.

Several more Amens followed before Mimi sang a solo. "In sempay-tair-na say-cue-lahhhh."

As she held the last note, Joe joined in with a drawn out "Ahhhhhh men."

Then Ray followed with another "in-sempay-tair-na say-cue-lahhh."

As the brothers held onto their note, Mimi resumed an Ahh-men.

This singing of parts at different intervals, like you sing the song row-row-row your boat, continued until they came together and harmonized a succession of Ahh-mens. Finally came the chorus.

"In sempay-tare-na! In sempay-tair-na! In sempay-tare-na! In sempay-tair-na!"

More Ahh-mens followed, then finally three climatic ones in succession: "Ahh-men! Ahh-men!! Ahh-men!!!"

Uncle Teach finished with a flourish on the organ.

"Bravo!" Uncle Teach said.

"Dinner's almost ready," Grandma Lasagna called.

The Lasagna kids cheered.

"Now go help grandma set the table," Uncle Teach said.

Next to singing, eating was the Lasagnas' favorite pastime. Like Indians on the warpath, the Lasagna kids scampered into the kitchen.

"Charles," Uncle Teach said, "you come and sit down with me."

He stood in front of the table, which had a red and white checkered tablecloth, while Uncle Teach took a jug of red wine and a wine glass out of a cabinet that was behind the table.

"Go ahead, sit down, Charles." Uncle Teach said.

Teach poured himself a glass of wine. As the aroma of tomato sauce filtered in from the kitchen, Charles wondered if he were going to be able to taste the food. He certainly could smell it. He took a whiff and exhaled it with a hum.

In no time the table was set and Grandma Lasagna was bringing in plates of round bulging pouches called ravioli. Uncle Teach said that they were made by Grandma Lasagna herself. After Grandma sprinkled on some grated cheese, Charles cut a piece of ravioli and rolled it around in the sauce. He picked it up with his fork. It was steaming, and he blew on it. Then he put it into his mouth.

"Mmmmmm," hummed Charles, who could taste better now than he ever could before: the sauce, the thick, creamy cheese, the tender macaroni.

Everyone joined in with the hums, and they were going non-stop when Grandma joined them.

"Mmmmmmmmmmmmmmmmmm!"

Everyone except Mimi had seconds. She was saving room for the fa-sol-las. Grandma brought them out on a silver platter. They were dark chocolate mounds, shaped like crowns, whose chocolate coating covered marshmallow and chocolate cake. The bakery where Grandma worked, had baked them the day before.

While Uncle Teach and the Lasagna kids began devouring the crowns, Charles took a small nibble. It felt like air but the sweetest, richest air. Then Charles heard trumpets. Taking a larger bite, he heard the chocolate royalty proclaimed louder. With each bite, the taste grew richer, and as he munched in ecstasy, a policeman entered.

"Tee-dough," Uncle Teach called.

Tito Lorenzo was a squat man nearly as bald as Uncle Teach but a little younger and not as short.

"Hey, Teasto," Tito called to Uncle Teach.

Tito smiled as he waddled in and patted Uncle Teach on the back. Grandma Lasagna moved her chair aside as Tito dragged an easy chair in from the living room. Charles stared at Tito who glanced around the table until he caught Charles's gaze.

"So, uh, Charles, how ya doing?" he said and shook Charles's hand. "Well, don't ya worry. We'll getta ya back home. I promise."

Tito and Uncle Teach got up from the table and went through the archway into the area off the living room. They were whispering.

"You like the fa-sol-las, Charles?" Grandma Lasagna asked.

Charles nodded then bit into his second cookie and gobbled it down. He wondered what Uncle Teach and his friend were talking about. Something must be wrong. Finally, they returned to the table.

"You want some coffee, Tee-dough," Grandma Lasagna asked.

"Sure," he said.

"Well, Charles," Uncle Teach said, "we've got good news for you. You can stay here tonight, okay?"

"Ok," Charles said.

"Tee-dough says the police are looking for your parents right now, so it shouldn't be long before they find them."

Charles remembered being down by the river with the Tongue and the shock of lightning that thrust his head against that tree. He also remembered meeting Hawenneyu and everything else that followed. But why had he ended up here with the Lasagnas?

"By the way, uh, Charles," Tito asked. "Coulda you give me the lasta names of somma your relatives because we canna find anyone witha the name Paganono. Maybe, uh, the lasta name of your mother's parents, or somma your aunts or uncles or cousins?"

"Well, there's Grandma and Grandpa Capellini," Charles said, "and my Uncle Vince Cacciatore, and then there's my cousins, the Tortellini's and the Linguini's, and my great Aunt Manicotti."

Tito raised his eyebrows at hearing the list, and looked at Uncle Teach, who shrugged.   "Now, uh, Charles," Tito asked, "whatta abouta your home-uh-town? Are you uh sure it's a called Haneckhadee?"

"Yes, of course."

"Wella, try uh hard to remember, Charles. There are so many uh towns and cities, and we needa to know the exacta name. Is it uh near Metro City?"

"Metro City?" Charles asked.

"Yes, donna you know Metro City?"

"No, where's that?"

There was a pause. Tito, Teach, and Grandma all looked at one other with raised eyebrows.

"You're inna Metro City, Charles," Tito said. "This is uh Metro City."

"But what about Windy City?" Charles asked. "You've heard of Windy City, haven't you? I mean just this afternoon, I was watching the Windy City Dandies play at Dandy Stadium. Windy City is in the same state where I live."

"Butta Charles," Tito said, "the Dandies, they play inna Metro City."

Charles's heart thudded. No wonder he couldn't get Uncle Vince's number -- he wasn't in Windy City. He thought that maybe he was somewhere Windy City didn't even exist. But how could that be? He had seen Nicky Noodle, hadn't he? Tito finished his coffee and grabbed a fasolla for the road.

"I'll see uh what I canna do, Charles," Tito said then looked at Uncle Teach. "I'll call as soon as uh I find outta something. Bye, uh, everybody."

The Lasagna kids were excited. Now Charles would be able to go to church with them in the morning and hear them sing. Though Charles felt confused, he at least could watch TV. He seldom watched it at home, but his parents didn't have cable anyway, so it wasn't a big deal. The Lasagnas had everything: cable, HBO, the Disney channel, the Sci-Fi channel, ShowTime, Cinemax. They even picked up channels sometimes from a nearby satellite dish.

Grandma Lasagna made up the sofa in the TV room for Charles to sleep on. While she did this, Charles and the Lasagna kids put on their pajamas. When they were ready for bed, she turned on the TV for them.

Charles liked old movies about cowboys and Indians, but the Lasagna kids persuaded him to watch a horror show hosted by a scary looking old guy with a weird voice, short white hair, and big shoulders. It didn't matter to Charles because he was sleepy. Tonight's show, the weirdo promised, would be a "thriller." Haunting music was followed by the crackle of lightning.

Charles's vision blurred. He didn't know if the ghoulish vision was part of the TV program or a dream. But it was coming, and it was red, round, and shiny. A tomato with a mouth opening and shutting. And huge. The size of an elephant. It bellowed. Charles ran. He thought it smelled like tomato sauce, of garlic, basil, oregano, like Grandma Lasagna's. He ran faster. But the tomato was gaining. Charles stopped and turned to face it. Up he grew. So big did he become that the tomato was no longer like an elephant but just a regular tomato. Charles grabbed it and took a bite, and the ground beneath him dropped, causing him to fall into a void -- blank, white, unending.

He tumbled end over end like a body lost in space, shooting down-down-down until he hovered over a spotlit stage. On it were a pianist and an orchestra. But only the pianist was playing. Charles floated closer. It was his father.

"Doom, doom, duh-doom, doom … duh-doom, duh-doom, duh-doom."

Charles recognized the music. He looked into the audience and felt himself pulled forward until he was suspended over the front row. Though dark, he saw his mother, Mindy, and her parents. His mother wore a long black dress, Mindy black pants and a black blouse. He moved closer. He could see their tears. But they couldn't see him.

"DOOM, DOOM, DUH-DOOM, DOOM . . . DUH-DOOM, DUH-DOOM, DUH-DOOM."

The music was quiet and went along like someone dragging a heavy weight. Charles noticed how sorrowful faces of the musicians were.

"DOOM, DOOM, DUH-DOOM, DOOM . . . DUH-DOOM, DUH-DOOM, DUH-DOOM."

Then, the music shifted into a quiet patter of tear drops. Tenderly, his father played the delicate music which was like a bittersweet dream. But it soon gave way to that grave passage Charles seemed to have known all his life.

"Doom, doom, duh-doom, doom . . . duh-doom, duh-doom, duh-doom."

The heavy refrain continued, and for the first time, Charles could feel the emotion his father felt when he was playing. His father's body seemed to tense up as he pounded the final note and held it as long as he could.

"Doom, doom, duh-doom, doom . . . duh-doom, duh-doom, duh-dooooooooommmmmmmm."

Charles's father fell forward on the keyboard. There were gasps from the audience, then silence, and finally deafening applause. But his father didn't move.

"Charles!" he heard a distance voice. "Charles!! Get up, Charles!"

Chapter Twenty-Six
And He Shall Rest in Peace

"Get up, Charles, get up," Mimi called.

He opened his eyes.

"It's time to go to church," she said.

Charles's excitement woke him right up. He was looking at Mimi's happy smile when Ray's ghostly figure came into the room. Dressed in his white choir gown, Ray carried a hanger with a powder-blue suit. The sun shone through a window, and the puffed-up shoulders of Ray's gown reminded Charles of wings, making him look like an angel.

"Hurry up, Charles," Ray said. "We have to get there early, so we gotta get going right away."

He laid the suit across the foot of the sofa.

"This is for you to wear, Charles. It's my favorite suit."

Ray led Charles through the kitchen where Grandma Lasagna was drinking coffee.

"It's getting late, Charles," she said.

Charles reached for the doorknob of the bathroom, and though he couldn't feel it, he could turn it. But the bath water was just the right temperature. He sank into it, and there came a thump on the door.

"Hurry up, Charles," Uncle Teach said.

When they left for church, Charles felt more and more apart from everything, like a distant radio station that comes in and fades out. They pulled into the parking lot of the huge, silvery gray Cathedral, and he looked up at the two steeples in front, and the grand steeple in the rear, whose cross seemed to pierce the sky. How insignificant it made Charles feel.

The Cathedral was elaborate. At various spots around the roof were gargoyles, lion-like demons with wings, and every part of the Cathedral seemed to point to heaven.

Below, along the stone sidewalks leading to the entrance, were rows of shrubs and garden flowers. Behind them were plots of grass with patches of blooming dandelion. People were shuffling in.

While Uncle Teach and the Lasagna kids went around back, Charles followed Grandma Lasagna who was entering through the front. But before he entered, he heard a faint voice.

"Charlie."

The voice sounded familiar.

"Over here, Charlie, over here."

Charles stopped, and looked around and down in the direction of the voice, but all he saw were patches of dandelions. He looked up. Grandma Lasagna was gone. And just a moment ago, a line of people was hurrying into the Cathedral. But now he was alone.

"I'm down here, Charlie, down here!" the voice became louder. "Down here, Charlie!"

Charles could've sworn a dandelion squirmed. He bent closer, then down on one knee. His eyes focused. He noticed the long brown hair and the impish grin. He put his nose up to her.

"Windy, it's really you."

"Yes, it's me, Charlie. Ohh, I'm so glad to see you, Charlie. How did you get to be a boy again?"

"I'm not sure, Windy. I only just remembered, just now, that we were together," he said and stopped when he thought he heard the singing again and wondered why Grandma Lasagna had left him. "It's hard to tell what's really happening, and what I think is happening. Even you, sometimes. I even think you're just something from out of my mind."

"Well, believe me, I'm not, Charlie. I'm here and I'm alive, and I'm real, just like you. Everything's alive, Charlie, everything!"

"But am I ever going to get back home? Am I Windy, am I?"

"I don't know, Charlie. But don't worry. As a flower, I've come to realize that everything happens as it's meant to be. And in the end we all go back where we came from, we all finally rest in peace."

Charles didn't understand. And it sounded now as if the singing were calling him.

"Don't worry, Charlie, everything'll be all right," Windy said. "Trust me, I know it will."

Charles felt the wind blow. The singing grew louder and he gazed at Windy, who smiled and started to say something when a sudden gust swept him off his feet as if he again were a dandelion seed. Flying backwards, he waved good-bye to Windy as he was ushered through open doors into the Cathedral.

The choir was in the balcony and the orchestra just below. Every seat was filled. A bass drum boomed once, twice, three times, four! The voices of the choir reverberated.

Charles zoomed up near the ceiling. He looked down. Burning candles created shadows of the faithful praying, and everywhere were crosses, statues, gold engravings, and stained glass. Alongside murals of old men with beards and serious expressions, he began to understand the strange language of the choir.

> Day of Judgment has come.
> Heaven, Earth, One Again,
> Flesh Will Be as Air
> Universe ....
> Cosmos ....
> Incomprehensible!

Charles looked across and saw Uncle Teach conducting. He also noticed someone from the choir wave. It was Ray. He wondered why Ray was with the choir and he was up in the ceiling with all the saints and the goodness that was God.

The choir grew quieter, fading into a whisper, and the orchestra took over. A trumpet played a quiet fanfare.

Another answered, and another. They blended. The trumpet soloed, and again the three blended. They grew louder. Louder and louder. They blared. Boom went the bass drum, and the vibrations bounced off the ceiling and surrounded Charles.

> All over the universe
> Trumpets sounding
> Love resounding
> Spirits dancing
> The jubilee
> Gabriel blows his horn
> Golden tones
> Enchant the souls
> In ecstasy

Charles felt as if in a tilt-a-whirl of music. Repeatedly, the fanfare was followed by verses of the choir, which danced up the shivering Cathedral walls and met at the topmost point of the huge dome ceiling.

> Trumpets sounding
> Love resounding

The sounds swirled around him, making him dizzy. The faithful in the pews below became a blur that looked like one person.

Ree-ee-ee-eenging!

The velvet vortex velocified. The air erupted beneath him. He shot up into a golden mist, sailing through space in free flight, enveloped in something he could feel but not see. A peaceful ease passed over him. It was as if he had fallen asleep and only knew utter, gray, silence.

When the mist cleared, he was close to the ground, outside the gates of a cemetery. Flowers of all kinds swayed, and flurries of puffballs cavorted. Charles floated above a row of plots then up a small incline. A bird descended towards him, a rodent scurried through the tall grass, a spider spun a web in a crevice at the tombstone's corner, and a hopper was caught in it. Standing upon the freshly dug earth was a newly glazed stone with his name artfully chiseled into it: Charles Patrick Paganono (1984-1995), beloved son of Peter and Helen.

A voice suddenly boomed: Most majestic and mellifluous master!

The puffballs parachuted to the ground. There was silence . . . A tiny bug, with flickering lights, buzzed around.

"Charles," a little boy's voice called as if over the intercom that his principal Leaning Head Louie used.

Charles recognized it but wasn't sure from where.

"You made it, Charles. You've finally made it!"

Charles couldn't see anyone.

"Charles, don't you know who I am?" said the voice, which came from the firefly.

"I'm you in kindergarten, and now I'm a firefly."

Charles didn't understand.

"You've made it, Charles, don't you realize it?"

Made it where? Charles wondered.

"To that place where everything is and always will be," the firefly answered. "There's nothing to worry about now."

The firefly's light flickered out and everything became black and silent. Charles sensed that he had become inert, unconscious, less than asleep. Then came the last nightmare. A bass drum boomed once, twice, three times, four! The choir shrieked in frightening harmony.

How he trembles
Quakes with terror.
Face to Face
With his resting place
He leaves nothing
But his remains

Charles's spirit shot up, a whirling dervish heading in a definite direction, a chase of notes booming with percussion, a minute entity encompassing all and nothing, streaking like a bolt of lightning -- sizzling, thrashing, exploding across the sky. Now Charles had become like the pinpoint of a diamond, pure and sparkling. He was not merely frightened but mystified. Could it be that he would never return home? He drifted as he listened to quiet singing.

> Let perpetual light,
> Shine upon him,
> The light
> That gave him life,
> Will yet shine
> On in the Darkness
>
> Rest in peace . . .
> Remember him.

> Ahh-men

Deliver me, Lord, from everlasting death and mourning on this joyful day of freedom for my immortal soul.

Charles soared and took his rightful place. In time that is everlasting, he ascended to his niche within the great cycle that makes up everything. It had been waiting for him, and as he glided, he heard cheers and, to his surprise, familiar voices.

"Hey, it's the fiddlefarter!"

"Charlie!"

"Cha-ya-ya."

" 'Tis now which means forever, lad!"

"We've been waiting for you, my darling Cha-la-la."

"No one deserves it more than thee, Tonto."

Then, three sweet notes played on an invisible synthesizer.

"Now, 'tis your turn, Tonto."

"But I can't play," said Charles, who could see nothing but darkness.

"Of course you can. You have come to that place where everything is possible."

Somehow, though he couldn't see the synthesizer, he played the melody.

"It's time now, Tonto."

"For what?" Charles asked.

"To become part of the orchestra."

A swirl of colors streaked over them like a flying saucer and materialized. It was Hawenneyu.

His hair had whitened; his cheeks grown wizened. He smiled.

"You have done well, little brother," he said in a voice raised higher by the years. "You have completed what was required. Now you can lie back in the lap of the Master of Life."

The old Indian looked upward, his eyes aglaze as down from the heavens came a little man. He had dark thinning hair with shards of gray strewn through. He was old but looked very young and carried himself like someone half his age. He thought it was about time he revealed himself. Even though he couldn't sing very well, he decided he would:

Feel the vibe
That makes us
Smile and laugh.
No longer,
Will
Never
Ever
Be.

Grab ahold.
Sing songs
Get down on it.

A joy
To be
With you
Forever now.

Let us
Chant
Together

Eternally

Hi-doh

Hi-Dee Ha-Ha

Hi-doh

Hi-dee.

The forms of Hawenneyu and the old man vanished, and there was humming. The music took Charles up into a great circuit of lights that resembled a constellation of stars, and each star was one of his friends. It was like they were playing ring around the rosy. Louder and louder, in great surging passages, beginning and ending at different intervals, intertwining with one another, they sang. Then Charles thought he heard the three notes, and they began to sing them, over and over.

Suddenly, Charles noticed each note spoke a word. He couldn't say them or spell them. No. It was something much better. He had become them. In majestic fanfares they rang into the distance.

Tom Calarco

GLOSSARY
Language of Yappiness

yache	take	yoin	join
yack	back	yole	hole
yady	lady	yollowed	followed
yaey	may	yoly	holy
yake	make	yome	come
yalled	called	yomet	comet
yan	can	yomm	some
yanguage	language	yommone	someone
yappen	happen	yommyay	someday
yappening	happening	yoncentrate	concentrate
yappiness	happiness	yone	done
yappy	happy	yonely	lonely
yariation	variation	yong	gong
yarvelous	marvelous	yonsonant	consonant
yass	pass	yon't	don't
yast	fast	yood	could
yaster	master	yor	for
yather	gather	yord	word
yatter	matter	yore	more
yav	have	yorever	forever
yawtch	watch	yorld	world
yay	day	yorry	worry
ya-yay	way	yort	sort
yaye	say	yost	most
yew	to	yot	not
yewe	do	yothing	nothing
yewyay	today	youble	double
yizz	fizz	yould	would
yo	so	yourney	journey
yocus	focus	yourse	course
yody	body	yow	now
yoe	go	yowel	vowel
yoh	no		

Tom Calarco

www.ingramcontent.com/pod-product-compliance
Lightning Source LLC
Chambersburg PA
CBHW070218030726
47505CB00006B/1726